a
rock
a
river
a
street

A Rock, A River, A Street

STEFFANI JEMISON

Primary Information

I used to prefer making my way in silence, but on certain days, a little comfort is called for.

I headed outside, grabbing a baseball cap and a giant pair of headphones, the kind that look like Mickey Mouse ears, for company.

When I leave my house, I have a few options: I can walk north, into and around Highland Park and the Ridgewood Reservoir.

I can walk south, toward Brownsville.

I can walk east, into Cypress Hills and Forest Park.

I can walk west, toward Ocean Hill and Stuyvesant Heights.

Today was a southeasterly day.

The adolescent trees—knock-kneed and skinny, bent in the wind—and the streets were mostly empty, except for a dignified man drinking Snapple in the doorway of the corner store a few blocks down.

In the haze, the pocket parks looked especially lush.

I found myself on a street I had never seen before. This happens sometimes when I run (I'm a runner), and even when I walk. I like to wander, zigzagging between one block and another, turning to avoid stopping at traffic lights, crossing to avoid rats or broken glass, to see a funny crumbling cornice or fresh playground or industrial mystery until I find myself deep in the heart of the borough, landlocked and quite alone, and I turn myself around and walk home again without a map.

So I wander to clear my head, walking slowly with no particular focus.

Sometimes closing my eyes and opening them every fourth step.

Sometimes trying to alternate the foot that touches the crack in the sidewalk.

Sometimes looking up at the sky and marking distance by the clouds, or by the trees.

Sometimes dragging my hand along a fence or a wall and feeling contact with a painter who felt contact with Barack Obama or Basquiat or Biggie or some notable man or woman from the neighborhood who died and was reborn on these walls.

I think, sometimes, about how the mural happens, about how grieving mothers and brothers and homies, collecting money, asking if B, the one who's such a good painter, he did the mural outside the Key Foods on Euclid, couldn't he come by and paint something for us to remember Antwaun.

Couldn't he use this picture, Antwaun's favorite, as a reference, couldn't he make something to show Antwaun alive and benevolent and warm in his own neighborhood, we can't just leave him stranded at the graveyard surrounded by other graves, covered in grass, cared for by strangers. He needs to be here with us.

At least this is what I was imagining as I touched Antwaun's cheek, his black rimmed eyes and toothy grin.

I was thinking: this copy will live forever, or at least as long as this wall remains on this corner and really even longer, because it has probably been photographed hundreds of times, I'm sure. It might even live in the catalogue raisonné of this graffiti artist who might go on to be the next Basquiat or Haring or, hell, I don't want to name the artists who started as taggers, I don't want to give them away.

It's not unreasonable is it, to wonder if the painting might live more vividly, and in more minds, and for more time than Antwaun himself, who seems to have been barely more than a child when he died.

Antwaun. He is a stranger to me but he also feels like a beloved, like when the pastor calls the flock beloved, a kind of intimacy that requires no explanation because God's love is a glaze that covers us all.

I thought about glazing and glass and sheens and thin skins as I moved alongside the wall, grazing it with the four tips of my fingers and the edge of my nail.

And then a little paint came off under my nail—I had pressed a little too hard—and I stared at it.

I had a piece of Antwaun on me, I thought, and wondered what to do with the paint. I decided to just keep it, walk around with scraps of brown and blue under my nails, to think of that not as dirt but as a boy, to see how that felt.

I unsoftened my gaze. The mural was painted on the long side of an enormous grocery store, the kind you drive to and park at, where people shop like they do in the suburbs, with carts and so much cereal and 12-packs of bottled water and stacks of frozen dinners and walk-in coolers of dairy and meat.

As I opened my eyes wider, taking it in, I found myself a few paces behind two girls dressed exactly alike—high ponytails with a black fountain of hair that flowed to their waists, tube dresses in a retro stripe, flashes of gold.

They walked similarly but not identically, and as they stepped, one gliding, languid, the other shorter, muscling along, I realized that they were probably not even biological sisters, much less twins.

The one on the left was taller, with a golden tint to the back of her neck. I strained to catch a glimpse of her face.

The girls were heading to the entrance and I followed right behind. The doors were not automatic—this was East New York, after all—and as one turned slightly sideways to bump her hip and shoulder on the glass, I could see her profile: false lashes, her upturned nose, maybe a hint of reddish freckles, a thick beauty mark that from my position, a few meters back, may or may not have been pasted on.

A rush of cold air startled me—I almost walked into a display of seasonal fruit—and I grabbed a basket, ready to pretend to look at produce as I kept an eye on the girls. But fresh vegetables were not what these girls had in mind—no, they kept walking, turned a corner, and now I could see that the other girl also had red freckles, also had a beauty mark, on the same side. It must be painted then, right? If they were twins it would be symmetrical? So they were not twins after all, but copies.

I followed them down one aisle and up another. They browsed condiments, picked mayonnaise.

They looked at cereals, grabbed at least four kinds.

They got hot dogs and ground chuck.

They got Hamburger Helper and frozen hash browns and Bisquick.

They both got one jar each of Welch's grape jelly and Mott's applesauce.

Their carts were identical, and they even placed their items in identical ways, so they had identical, precarious stacks, like carbon copies.

And all the time I was surreptitiously following them, copying but with a difference. I picked fruit punch instead of applesauce, Eggo waffles instead of hash browns, veggie sausage instead of hot dogs, and so on.

Then they were up at the front of the store, ready to check out. I didn't know if they had seen me.

I put my basket on the floor near the conveyor belt, raised my hands just a bit to prove to the cashier that I wasn't stealing anything, shrugged an apology, mumbled something about forgetting my wallet, squeezed into the narrow checkout lane with the girls—there was no way out but *through* in this place—and wriggled myself past them both, close enough to smell their musky vanilla perfume and Lady Speed Stick, close enough to see the stray hairs in their glossy lipstick, close enough to feel their big bones and skeptical glares, as I pushed past and didn't look back.

I kept walking—past the mural, past the grass, past the park, past the railroad tracks, past the big houses, past the library, past the YMCA, past the front door, up the stairs, into my apartment.

I washed my hands and carefully scraped Antwaun, the pieces of him I carried, into the sink.

I pulled out my sketchbook and tried to remember every detail. Now I was drawing one girl, now I was drawing another. I looked at my marks. So now there were four, two in life and two on the page. I wondered which would last longest.

Maybe you have to be two so that you can have an extra, in case one dies, or so that you can persist as long as possible in as many minds as possible. Maybe I too needed to be two.

~

The film begins with a wide-angle view of a city park. Not my park, but a different one in a different city, perhaps San Francisco or Washington, DC or Boston or even midtown Manhattan. Maybe London, maybe Berlin.

The picture is diagrammatic, architectural, busy. Each person has a shadow that's so much more substantial, in this overhead angle, than the little bodies themselves, which almost disappear. Everyone coalesces and glides in predictable ways, like traffic. They sense the right places to connect and how close to get and the right places to diverge, and how far to go. Like blood races, coalescing in arteries and veins and separating into skinny capillaries at the edges and then coming back together again.

As the camera gets closer, my attention is drawn to a man who doesn't belong. It's not his clothing or his face or his body—I can't quite make out any of these—but rather his movements. Somehow he seems to be oriented outward, like the pinball in a machine, or a pool ball, bouncing from one body to another before springing free, ricocheting between people with reckless abandon, and it feels as though he is wrecking something like the self-contained energy we take for granted as we move in public spaces; he is invasion everywhere he turns, merely because he is paying attention when you would prefer to be left alone.

He is doing that mime thing—pretending he's pulling a bystander toward him as the person walks along, minding his business, then pretending to be dragged after him as though tethered by a rope.

He imitates the walk of one man, exaggerating the swagger, but stops when the guy threatens to hit him.

He ricochets toward a nearby cluster of men, the camera is much closer now, then stands next to another man and imitates his posture, bringing his hand to his mouth as the man brings his hand to his mouth to drink a sip of coffee.

The man takes a few steps away, quickens his pace, and is followed by the mime, who refuses to be shook.

The man, practically running now, is clearly uncomfortable and I wonder why—surely this is harmless—but then I realize the movie has begun, and he has very good reason not to want attention drawn to his movements, his gestures, his being. He is trying to hide and the pantomime, doubling his actions, is not only making him *not* invisible but actually amplifying his presence.

I press pause. More than half the frame is in shadow, covered or darkened by some object outside the frame, presumably a skyscraper although it could just as easily be a mountain or a meteor. The line between sunny and shaded is sharp. From this view, it appears as though there were a monster, just out of view. The monster might be a plane, or Godzilla, or a spaceship, or even a really dense cloud. It is most likely a building, in negative.

I am thinking about the relationship between positive and negative forms. My chair, for example, as a negative form of my backside. The pencil by my journal on the bedside table, a straight line, a negative form of the straight line from the page through the narrow and intimate space between my fingers. The journal itself, a negative form of my self, a scrawled and sprawling representation of what my skull so neatly contains.

I close my eyes. The scents are vague: maybe a little lemon, a little trash, a little foot, a little stale, a little mold, a little popcorn. Negative forms? Proof of life?

At some point in the evening, I take off my socks—"like a baby," my mother used to say with a frown. She always wore slippers to protect some kind of energy; her bare soles never touched the floor.

The bottoms of my own feet were always ruddy, lint between my toes, picking up everything I had touched. Unclean, I know my mother thought, even though the uncleanliness is everywhere, I told her, my feet recording rather than producing the soil.

On the oriental rug: two black pools, negative forms of each foot, deflated and deformed.

There is no weather in this room; is that negative? Is that positive? I cannot feel my skin. I can sense, though, the electric glow of the screen, and I can hear its crackling and rustling. I cannot feel any bones at all.

I try to remember the last time I was not aware of my shins. I wonder if negativity is a method of healing, or if healing has to be positive. I wonder if healing is always a mess, or if it can be clean. Will healing be more like an emptying or a filling? Like a thickening or a thinning? Will it be like watching a pot boil? Will I be able to feel it at all?

My arm was bent across my body, my hand grasping my shoulder like a clamp, like an embrace, and the shoulder was a positive and the hand was a negative, or the shoulder was a negative and the hand was a positive.

I turned around. The light from the television was just enough to produce a shadow, larger and more indistinct than me, on the blank white wall behind my couch.

I turned back to the screen and pressed play. Get lost, someone is saying to the pantomime. Beat it.

Like the kids say: I know you are but what am I?

~

Like
like

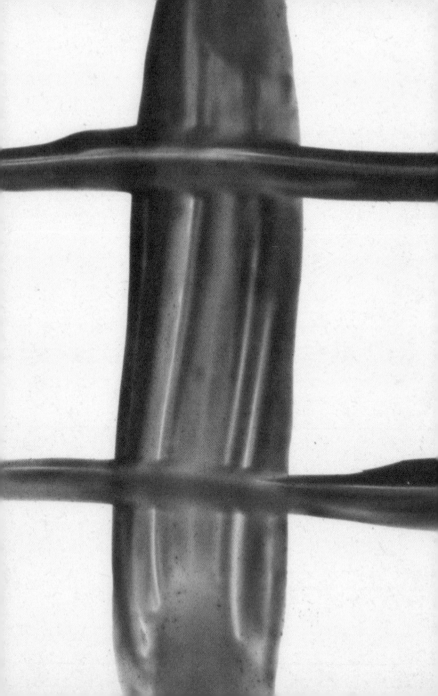

Most of the time I stayed close to home. My walks and my runs were my radius; I rarely needed to go further.

But today I had stumbled into the subway, exhausted, and collapsed into a seat, the back of my head slumping against a window, my body facing an identical row in front of an identical window on the other side of the car.

An older man occupied the middle seat across the way, which meant that when I gazed forward, I could see my own face reflected in the glass as well as this man's face right next to it, side by side. He was looking intently at a folded newsprint magazine; even from this distance of—what, eight? nine feet?—I could see that thick bifocals or trifocals splintered and magnified his eyes into horizontal shards. His creamy skin was crowned by a plume of longish white hair, longer than you would imagine for a man who was clearly in his eighties or nineties, the kind of haircut that was popular for movie stars when I was younger, a River Phoenix haircut or Jordan Catalano haircut, loosely pushed back, which gave him a kind of dashing look even as I knew that the hair was probably elaborately planned to cover a bald spot that, at his age, must be inevitable—why hide it? why not be grateful to be alive at all? Nonetheless he looked rakish, with his legs crossed elegantly and his rumpled white shirt and his tweed jacket and platinum chain watch, which he laid the paper down to consult more than once as I watched him.

A watch! On a chain! Does he even have a cell phone, I wondered, then chided myself—everyone has a cell phone, especially old men who ride the subway alone. Especially men like this who, while admittedly elderly in some contexts, are not an unusual sight in New York. Maybe if he lived in Ohio or Kansas he would bunk in the guest room with his grown daughter and her husband and wear khakis and be a little less independent, or even be a rakish, long-haired presence at an assisted living facility, because I have noticed that people seem to need only the assistance that is not already given, or he could live in Florida with other older people, where he might wear a visor or sunglasses, and shorts as he reads on the beach, perhaps joined by a companion). But here, in New York, even men beyond a certain age wake up alone, and dress alone, and read the newspaper alone in the company of others at Old John's or Sarabeth's or Barney Greengrass or another favorite, and they sit on park benches, looking at birds and relaxing, their legs crossed, thinking of everything they have seen from this very bench in Central Park over so many years and decades before, and they go to the theater alone or with an old work colleague, perhaps the one who was assistant editor or editorial assistant when the man was editor-in-chief, somebody twenty or thirty years younger, still young enough to remember the gentleman in his prime—or is he now in his prime?—and alone is something he generally does very well indeed, just as he thinks he has done everything well since he was a child—well he must have done, because look how well the world had done for him!

It is reciprocal, isn't it? You get out what you put in? I bet he'd bet his life on it.

I crossed my left leg over my right as I watched him and allowed my hands to drift into the position of his, my head to cock to the side, my squint to slowly and subtly (I thought) emerge from the blankness of my face.

Diagonally across from me was a boy, no more than twenty, with a five- or six-year-old child on his lap and a finger in his mouth, staring at me intently. I ignored him—I always ignore the stares of small children—but didn't forget him.

Now that I was being observed, I was aware that I was not subconsciously mirroring the man, but rather participating in a kind of performance, a relay, the old gentleman on display, channeled into me on display for this kid.

The kid looked at me and at the gentleman, back and forth a few times. The gentleman had not looked up once—I doubt he could have seen me if he had—do trifocals see that far?—and I had never stopped looking at him.

Man. Newspaper. Me. Man. Child. Me.

We looked and looked like this until, after a few stops, the kid crossed his legs too, opened his hands as if holding the *New York Review of Books*. He smiled at me.

His dad looked down, noticing the shift in weight, and then shot a suspicious glance in my direction. *Who are you smiling at*, I felt was what he wanted to say, but instead he gave the kid a little love slap, "What are you doing?" he said to the kid. "Here, take this," and gave him his phone. The kid shook his head, grinning bigger, more impertinent now, and the dad said, "Stop."

Now a few people around us looked up, and one of them saw something in me, I could tell. He didn't do anything, but looked at me hard. My stop was next and when I stood, he followed.

"Hey," he said as I walked faster up the stairs, ignoring him. "Hey," he said louder, then started to bound up, two at a time. I began to run—raced through the turnstiles and up the last flight and into the street, which was empty, as it often was at this station at this time.

The man pushed my shoulder and I was too petrified to yell. I was summoning my inner self, I was about to say, "What do you want" very calmly, holding my tote bag with two hands, but I didn't have to say anything because he took a step back. He gazed at me for a moment, confused, then turned around. "I thought you were someone else," he muttered as he walked away.

A few months ago, my lower legs began to hurt. At first, the discomfort started four or five miles in, just after I had begun my return. I would keep stuttering along, almost limping, gritting my teeth and thinking about ice and peace and flowers.

I began to shorten my path by half, often not making it out of the neighborhood, making a short loop at Jamaica Avenue or skipping the steep hill to the park, feeling pathetic and partial.

But recently the pain had been creeping up earlier and earlier until I could feel it almost as soon as I left, a sharp stabbing that flattened into an aching that haunted me, like a ghost, for the rest of the day. Running being a collection of jolts to one foot and then the other, a series of thousands and thousands of hard, little landings.

Any expert worth her salt would tell me to stop, which I did not intend to do. But one day, last week, I felt my leg crumbling from the very first step. I realized suddenly I might have to make a choice between not running now or not running ever again.

Sitting upright on the bed, bags of iced peas on each shin, I scrolled through my laptop looking for an orthopedist with a kind name. I filtered out the ones near me—I'd seen the bitter faces rushing in and out of the hospital nearby—and decided to focus on Manhattan. I wanted somebody young and sympathetic—no Oscars or Arthurs—and eventually landed on the guy. Joshua turned out to be a young man, just a few years older than me, a former Division 1 football player who didn't question my unequivocal requirement that any treatment plan enable me to keep running, but did gently tell me, after X-rays, that my shin splints had already led to stress fractures in both shins, which had caused adaptations up and down the "chain," from my feet to my pelvis and even my arms.

"It's up to you," he said, drumming his fingers on a greige laminate "desk" as I took notes in my notebook.

Up you, I wrote.

"If you take a few weeks off," he told me, "you might be able to save your hip."

Hip slip, I wrote.

"If you take a few months off," he said, "you might still be running in ten years."

Take off, I wrote.

"Have you tried cycling," he asked?

I didn't bother writing that one down.

He sent me home with a prescription: no high impact exercise. No jumping, no running. Reduce the load that my shins are supposed to support. "And I don't mean that you should lose weight," he added, as if he could read my thoughts.

I walked lightly down the sidewalk, past mature trees and stout brick houses and peeling vinyl siding and carefully tended, hard-won front gardens.

I stepped, breathing so deeply I was almost holding my breath, then letting it all go in a whoosh, letting my shoulders fall, letting the tension dissipate, allowing myself to exaggerate that feeling of relaxation, as when you turn the water in the shower a little cooler, so that you can then turn it all the way up and make it scald. An illusion of heat. Tension, and then an illusion of release.

As I shrugged, I contemplated my next steps.

I wish I had never seen the X-ray, a hairline as thin as a squint barely segmenting what should be one lower leg bone into two, almost identical on both sides.

I asked for a copy of the images and was given a code to download them from an online portal. The first thing I did when I got home was enter the code and pull up the pictures. It was as though someone had taken a pencil to the photograph and drawn the very finest line.

My stomach knotted as I zoomed in, wondering if in fact what looked like a fracture could just be an aberration in the machine.

Should I get a second opinion? I turned it over. The diagnosis was nauseating, but strangely satisfying.

I listened to my shin for an ache. All I could feel was the rush of my blood.

I inspected my skin for a sign. It was clean, of course. Why white people never believe you when you tell them you are blushing or bruised.

I desired to squeeze my bones, the way you squeeze a papercut to make blood.

A Rock, A River, A Street

When I eat dinner I like to keep the television on. The
episodes of procedurals flow like water in a stream.
　　and order and law and order and law and order and
law and order and law and order and order and order
　　Have I mentioned that I find endlessness comforting?
One of my guilty pleasures is running water from the tap.

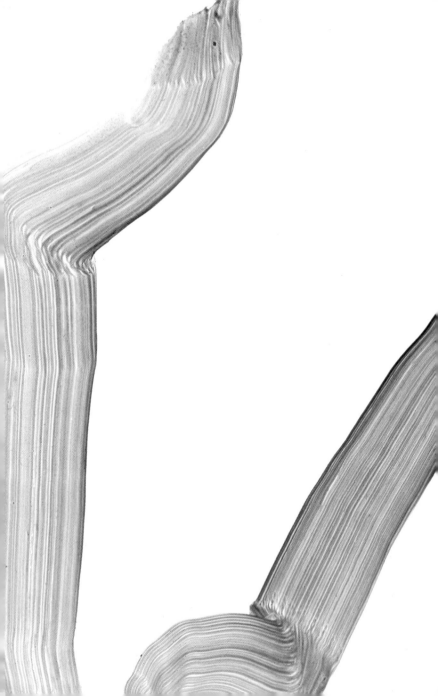

So we talk about risky behaviors like they're a specific collection, like it's risky to play with fire or walk on the highway or stand at the edge of a cliff, but the thing about risk is that it's actually a general condition.

I am always at risk of not existing, which is to say that no matter what I do or don't do, I am always only an accident or bad mood or bad trip or bad boyfriend or bad slip and fall from being pulled away or pushed away or taken away or just slipping and sliding away; it can happen any time.

Several times, I have been shoulder-to-shoulder with my own disappearance, and the experience was so big—certainly bigger than anything my own consciousness can absorb—that I still can't tell you exactly what happened.

~

I never used to be particularly observant.

My mother told me when I was a child that I always had my head in the sky. She could cut her hair or change her clothes and I wouldn't notice.

She once told me that someone else could have picked me up in her Dodge Caravan and I wouldn't even have noticed that she had been replaced. That might be true. Because in fact, I don't think we had a Caravan at all. I was never very good with cars.

I do know that I have always been more attentive to what I think is going on inside than to what is happening on the surface.

I have never quite understood "lying." There have always seemed to me to be only so many variations of truth.

When I was fifteen, I joined the cross-country running team. I had always avoided group activities, but I liked the idea of being able to outrun anyone. It felt like a useful escape skill, a useful life skill. I quickly found myself totally addicted, obsessed with running every day after school and every morning on my own.

What is interesting to me is negation.

If lying is impossible, you may ask, how do you throw up a flag, how do you misdirect intentionally, how do you tell people that something is wrong?

For me, the answer is withholding. It is no speech at all. Or it is to be positive, but in the wrong direction.

Like when you're running, flocking with a gaggle of girls and they go right and you turn left.

And it is three days before you make it home and when you arrive, everyone is confused because you refuse to speak, you have returned your voice to God and chosen another way to live.

What happened to you, they say, shaking your shoulders. *Where were you?* You have nothing to say.

⁓

My mother is religious. "I will make your tongue stick," she underlines in her copy of the *King James*, as though I am being punished for my sins, although she anguishes and skulks in her housedress, all synthetics and felt and elbows, as though she were the one who had sinned.

"I will make your tongue stick to the roof of your mouth"—and it's true that the stickiness is not in the lips—I imagine someone's cheeks puffing up like a blowfish—far too easy to poke. Stickiness is in the tongue, such a thick muscle, a thick and impermeable and uncomfortable barrier to the rest of my body.

My mouth can open but my tongue, furled and braced, can stay stuck.

They took me to the doctor and although I struggled they were able to pry open my lips. But they could not see past my tongue. They were stuck and so was I.

They wrenched open my jaw by threatening to break it. "We do it all the time," the doctor claimed, a grim look on his face. Something about lockjaw and incomplete healing. I didn't want a broken face. I didn't want that kind of pain. But my tongue, there was no medical reason to cut out my tongue. My tongue would stay.

⁓

When I stopped speaking, I had to also stop singing, of course. I would go to choir rehearsals on Tuesday nights and hum along, but I did not sing.

~

I kept running, although my parents wanted me to stop. I think they were afraid I would run alone. (I was done with the team and they were done with me.)

So I would run like a boxer, my dad in the car next to me, driving stonily alongside and a little ways behind, as I ran around and around our subdivision in loops of 2.13 miles exactly.

~

I ate, but mostly privately, in the bathroom, in the bleachers, in the school hallways, in front of the TV, in the basement, in my room.

I chewed gum constantly when I was alone, a few packs a day, spitting one piece into the new wrapper of another like a chain smoker getting a fix.

~

I really can't tell you why I stopped. I just know that one day I closed my mouth and didn't feel a need to open it again.

At first, I sometimes thought I had something to say, but I swallowed my words and they never got past my throat, and it almost felt like they were growing and sticking in me, like peanut butter in your gullet, getting bigger and bigger but not blocking.

What I mean is that I could breathe, my mind remained clear, but I had something like a fly trap for my ideas so I could catch them one by one and hold them behind my lips so they didn't escape or get nasty.

I let the words stack up but after a while it started to feel less like a pile of gold I was sitting on that I could harvest any time, and more like a pile of dirty laundry rotting and getting stale the longer it lay in my insides without getting air or being refreshed. I started worrying that my mound of words would turn into literal trash.

I looked up "rotting ideas inside my body" and "can words hurt you" but found nothing of interest, only sticks-and-stones stuff. I knew better. I knew that words in the body are a real physical thing, made of breath and maybe blood and steam and carbon monoxide and whatever other poisons I exhale. That holding onto the words might be like holding onto a hurt, and I could find myself in real jeopardy, like widowers who die of a broken heart.

~

In Catholic school, we were forced to participate in what was called liturgical dance. Our teacher, an ethereal being with long feet and powdery blonde hair and too much eyeliner, wore wrap skirts and wrap sweaters and ribbons and delicate jewelry.

She taught us to make symbols with our fingers and wrists to say: "Lamb of God, you take away the sins of the world. Have mercy on us / grant us peace."

She used a contraption the length of her arm to set the votive candles aflame, lined up at the front of the altar. We would scurry toward them like little mice, scatter away with fire in our hands, feeling radiant. One particularly satisfying twirl ended with us standing in a line from tallest to shortest, each girl holding the candle, arms extended toward the next girl's back. I smelled the fire before I saw it. The neck of the girl in front of me was barely burned at all, but she had to cut three inches from her hair, which had once swung proudly below her butt.

I wore my hair in long braids in those days, the kind with crunchy ends that had been seared, one by one, with a cigarette lighter. But this girl's hair had sizzled, rather than melted. There was a little pile of ash on the ground where she stood.

I became acutely aware of how few ways my own body moved in the course of a regular day. I began making up dances in my room. I interpreted all of my favorite songs and poems. I pointed to myself when I meant "I." I spread my fingers wide. I practiced directing my gaze upward and outward. I incorporated lunges. I rolled my shoulders and my head. I took deep breaths. I leaped.

I watched DVDs of *Sleeping Beauty* and *Swan Lake* in my room. The ballerinas I saw on TV could rotate their legs from their hips like the seamless swivel of a bottle and a cap. They had the uncanny ability to bend in order to appear straight. Their ankles were not right angles, but could become flat as a ruler to create a single line from the end of the big toe to the crown.

I made my parents take me to see *The Nutcracker* twice that year, wearing the same baggy black velvet dress each time. I sat as close as I could afford and tried to hear the dancers breathe.

I created a setup with a full-length mirror in one corner and my TV in another, so I could see myself and the reflected television in a single surface. I recorded my choreography on my mother's camcorder, watching the videos carefully to find ways to improve.

After a time, I moved my activities from my bedroom into the basement, where I could spread out. I was still running daily, but I spent most of my running time practicing choreography in my head.

Over time I felt like I was developing quite a fluency. But at fifteen, I knew I was too late. I combed the internet for stories about dancers who were old when they started, but I knew it was rare. I read the affirmations ("It always seems impossible until it's done" and "There is nothing impossible to him who will try"); I also knew better than to believe them. I never counted on myself to be an exception, not ever.

On a whim, and secretly, I decided to submit a video audition to the dance program at a college in the city. I knew I wasn't trained but I didn't know if I needed to be. Maybe I had natural talent. My parents were confused when I told them what I would be studying, but I promised them that I would also be minoring in biology, that my intention was to become a physical therapist.

I wrote these things rather than speaking them. My parents and I communicated mostly by email. I was one of the first kids I knew with a cell phone. I sent SMS messages to them and sometimes even to myself, tapping each number on my Nokia to get a different letter. I became an expert in predictive text.

As the months passed, I became increasingly worried about where all that weird voice energy was going to go.

I had read in science class about how cow farts emit methane, literally cracking a hole in the sky, which seemed proof to me of the importance of actually releasing your waste from your body, because if it could burn a hole in the very atmosphere of the Earth, just imagine what it would do to a cow if unreleased. It could certainly burn a hole in a cow, it could certainly burn a hole in me.

I began drinking more seltzer to produce bigger belches. I even tried making myself vomit, although I wasn't at all sure if the contents of my lungs and the contents of my stomach were related. I cleared my throat often, but only when I was alone. I traced the alphabet with my tongue to give it an outlet. I started thinking about talking.

But the thing about a streak is that it's really hard to interrupt once you've gotten going. Because you get a little worried that the flow, once unleashed, will never stop.

I am a runner. I run every day, and it is less like the force of the wind or the gush of a river and more like the dribble of a hose that flows forever, but slowly.

It has been fifteen years? twenty? and I still don't speak much.

Like a hiker, I traipse. I keep my eyes forward, as if that could protect me.

I ignore the lawn-chaired corner store uncles in their ribbed tanks and high socks and baggy jean shorts and skin the color and texture of desiccated autumn leaves, I ignore their cigarettes and their weed ashes piled up, I ignore their bodega cats lying defiantly in the middle of my path.

I ignore all of the card games and all of the open car doors and all of the music. I ignore the midday clusters outside the liquor store and the sidewalk-blocking barbecues and the sidewalk-blocking children with soccer balls and scooters, whizzing by me before I even have a chance to "watch out," the delivery drivers who push past on electric scooters without a warning, no boundaries.

I ignore the cracks and crumbles and dimples and divots and straight-up holes in the sidewalk, the way they seem like they are falling apart all around me, everything is falling apart around me.

I ignore the flickers around the edges of my vision, which sounds poetic except that they are probably rats.

I ignore the men who slow down, offering me cards, offering me jobs, offering me dates, offering me compliments, I ignore the honking when I pass, I ignore the *tssssssst*-ing, I ignore the stares.

I ignore the cars parked on cement blocks, flat fixes extending their garage right through to the street, men balanced on their backs on dollies, wrenches in their hands, crowds of more men watching each other work. I ignore the men.

I would always be on the verge of toppling if I weren't such a good, such a truly expert walker, and I weave my way through and enter the big double gates that always reminded me of the entrance to a football stadium or parking lot, a "gated community" but of souls.

The place is haphazard, spreading in every direction, dotted with trees that bloom brilliantly in the spring and glisten and rustle through the fall and turn handsome and noble in winter and provide welcome, warm shade in the summer.

I'm making it sound wild, and it's not wild. It's a cemetery, fully operational: manicured and controlled, patrolled by black security vans, organized and mowed, more like a lawn than a meadow, perhaps something in between, something like a field. But the field is hollow, honeycombed, full of pockets that are coffins, as though when walking you might accidentally drop through, like a sinkhole, like a video game where you jump up and down and worry about falling. It's quiet, never more than a handful of people at a time.

The bodies are buried in clusters, organized by ethnicity, as though a family or a church or a block or a community bought a few hundred graves at a time, figuring they could decide later how to divvy things up.

Many of the headstones have round or oval rocks, smooth as oversized pebbles, balanced on each side of the curved top of the grave. I wonder what the stones mean as I wander from one path to another, never entirely sure if and when I am allowed to go "off road" so to speak, but figuring that by design, every grave in a graveyard should be accessible, so if I need to walk up one row and down another in order to get my steps in privately, I should be allowed to do that, even if I am one of very few people who ever steps off the path. When I walk I always wonder if people think I'm a mourner. I never know whether to meet the eyes of the people I pass.

I have never run in the cemetery. I don't know that I have a good reason, unless "it feels like the scene of a horror movie" is good enough. Too easy to imagine crowds of ghosts in pursuit, or a stalker hidden behind one of the giant crypts that lines the entrance. Even when I could run, I preferred to walk in the graveyard and run in the streets.

But sometimes I see neighborhood runners jogging through a cemetery path, because every runner hates stopping at red lights, and because in the midst of this endless green you can imagine that you are not clustered in the smoggy winter of the biggest city in the country, in the middle of an ugly post-industrial neighborhood dotted with shabby houses built for the mid-century middle class, but instead pretend to be a discoverer, a suburbanite, a freedom runner, breathing clean air and cushioned by green grass, okay if not suburban then maybe a dweller of some idyllic European city with dirt trails and rewilded zones and carefully managed doses of nature designed to optimize quality of life in an already impossibly clean and safe place, where everyone's basic needs are met.

The cemetery was fully operational, I saw piles of dirt and security vans and other indications of staff all the time. There were buildings scattered throughout, but they were always closed when I walked by, and I had no idea how to get in. I tried calling, but no one had ever picked up. I wanted to know how much it would cost to buy a plot.

I wore a school uniform nearly every day from kindergarten to my high school graduation. They varied somewhat from one school to the next—I moved between private schools and Catholic schools and back again—but they always involved plaid and pleats.

The uniforms were meant, I think, to erase the small distractions, the expense, the ornamentation, everything associated with fashion.

We were allowed to choose very few things: the type, but not the color, of our white or navy socks: folding, bobby, no-show.

The type of brown, black, navy, or white leather shoes, within a narrowly acceptable range of styles, sneakers excluded.

The type of collared white blouse, including the fit—baggy or narrow, the sleeve length, the cuff (if applicable), the material, and the type of collar.

The length of our skirts: nearly down to our knees, dowdy, or just below our fingertips, daring. The gap of a few inches felt cavernous then.

We could choose how to wear our hair: "down," "half-up, half-down," "up."

We could choose what kind of jewelry we wanted, with some limitations: gold and silver colors were permitted, small crosses and charms were permitted, fashion jewelry and costume jewelry were not, large jewels were prohibited, and so on.

As we moved into high school, I became something of an expert in the calf and shin area of other girls, it being one of the largest areas of exposed skin for most of us, revealing more than almost anything else of the actual contour and shape of the body.

The lower leg communicated whether the student was an athlete, more or less, although it could sometimes be wrong as some girls had congenitally large calves and others, small and thin ones.

It communicated whether the girl was capable of sitting, as all the cool girls sat, in a kind of bind, one thigh wrapped entirely around and twisted among the other, the twist bound by an outstretched foot, a maneuver that required both slender legs and a sturdy enough foot.

The lower leg revealed whether the girl shaved her legs or not, a matter of increasing significance as we got older. It was the gateway to other important questions, like what kind of socks she chose and what kind of shoe, and above, how long or short the skirt was.

One day, midway through the school year, midway through junior high, a new girl arrived. Often I noticed that visitors didn't quite understand the rules of the uniform; they were too eager to fit in and didn't notice the requisite small variations. They missed important details like choosing the right collar, the right cuff length, making sure the top button only was unbuttoned, failing to wear an appropriate tank underneath to create an appropriate silhouette.

The first mistake was often failing to have the skirt—which came long enough to hit most girls at the kneecap—hemmed to exactly the furthest extension of the pointer finger. The second mistake, which sometimes accompanied the first, was wearing the hair too carefully groomed. A neat ponytail, a French braid, a ballerina bun—these might work in other contexts, but when combined with the uniform, it made the overall look overly prissy.

But this new girl, a white girl like the rest of them, seemed to get it from the get go. She was somehow simultaneously absolutely one of us and our leader at the same time, at least sartorially.

I say "us" in the loosest possible sense. There was an "in-group," like in the movies, and there was everyone else. The groups were fairly static. The group of popular girls centered around one blonde, a soccer player whose older sister attended the same school and was part of the cool crowd in her own grade. It was the close presence of the sister, the proximity to boys from the boys' school and learner's permits and second, third, fourth-hand smoke and college tours and CK One, that rubbed off on the blonde, made her smell like cell phones and coffee. We called our in-group the N-group, after the blonde whose name began with an N, and the other chosen ones assembled around her like the lesser, decorative flowers in a bouquet.

There was one brown girl in the mix, a girl whose mother, an executive, was from India. We had heard they were of noble birth somehow, which is perhaps why this girl, the color of warm khaki with pink lips and very long lashes, was let in.

It wasn't cool to be dumb, not at an all-girls school, and the N-group kids played sports and were very good if not great students. I, too, was a very good if not great student, but I was not one of them. I was a student of the N-group and I knew what they needed and why I couldn't serve it. My lips were taupe, the color of brick, and not pink. My lower legs were so thick that I didn't bother to get the right socks. I didn't mind their perfection, and I still don't resent it. What's for them is not for me.

Before the new girl arrived, I often ate lunch alone, reading. But on her very first day, she glided next to me, placing her tray and pulling out a neatly packed lunch from a vintage looking case. Her foods looked somehow simple and exotic—tabbouleh salads, I later found out, and bright berry Kombuchas, and little drinkable yogurts, where the rest of us had milk, and little wedges of naan instead of regular bread. Everything in her box smelled like vinegar, and to this day, I think of vinegar as the most sophisticated acquired taste.

Her shirts were cotton and actually had to be ironed; none of the other parents would ever consider such a thing, not when permanent press was available. She wore a thick undershirt with spaghetti straps underneath, which gave her ensemble a softer, blurrier look. The rest of us wore athletic shorts under our skirts, causing them to puff out a bit rather than lay flat, but she wore biker shorts, creating a slimmer and more streamlined silhouette. We wore brown suede lace-up shoes, whereas hers buckled with a silver clasp. They made her feet curve softly at the toes, like a doll's rounded feet, as opposed to ours, which created longer, elliptical shapes. Her brown hair folded just below her ears—she was one of very few white women in school with short hair—and she had a coquettish little smile. She informed us that she had transferred from a school in Massachusetts, which sounded unfathomably sophisticated.

The other mothers had shoulder-length hair, but the new girl's mother had freckles and thin, long hair that swung down her back like a girl's. On days I didn't have track, she would pick us up after school—we'd change clothes in the bathroom—and leave us to wander in the mall. We could pretend to be independent—"I think I want a hot chocolate," for example, one of us might say—and it felt so grown up to make our own choices about what we wanted and didn't want in this place where every single option we could imagine was available to us.

I don't know why she picked me. Coming from another community, she might not have realized that I was wrong, and then might not have been able to figure out how to backtrack. The N-group at the time were mostly athletes, but the new girl didn't like to compete, so that may have been it. Or it may simply have been that the others were taken. Regardless, I was reluctantly, skeptically, dizzyingly grateful.

One day I left the new girl to pick through earrings at Claire's while I hurried to the bathroom. While I was doing my thing in the stall, I glanced at the gap and looked at the shoes and socks of the person next to me. Like I said, shoes and socks were a specialty of mine. I was an aficionado. The person was wearing skinny jeans and white Chuck Taylors. Somebody older than me, I decided. People my age can't keep white sneakers clean. The skinny jeans, though, meant they weren't too old. Maybe college? I wouldn't be able to guess people's ages with accuracy for decades.

I exited first. Then I heard a bionic flush—the mall toilets were so powerful, it always sounded like a space-ship landing every time you pressed the handle, so much so that I used to do it over and over again as a child, imagining I was getting beamed up and out of there like in *Back to the Future*—and she came out. I was genuinely surprised to see a girl my age. She had long hair, jet black and razor straight, and I couldn't stop staring as she used a thick, plastic, bright blue fingernail to adjust her part. Our eyes met in the mirror—she was wearing a full face of makeup with fake black freckles dotted with pencil. Her lashes were longer than any I had ever seen.

I realized she wasn't moving, and realized it was because I wasn't moving, and she was staring at me because I was staring at her.

I blushed my invisible blush and said "I like your

shoes" even though I couldn't even see her shoes—I had learned that directing attention downward was the only way to defuse the staring situations in which I so often found myself—and she said nothing but went back to her own grooming, businesslike and with purpose.

I remembered my hands, which had been soaping under the running water for what felt like minutes. By the time I looked up, she had left. I gazed at myself in the mirror with a fresh perspective.

Should I release my hair from the "messy bun" I wore every day, the bun like a sculpture that approximated the shape of the other girls' hair while hiding the fact that it was made of different stuff? I pulled off the band and watched the braids cascade lightly onto my shoulders. Did I look older? Did I look different? I combed through them with my fingers, tried to part them on one side to make an arrangement. I couldn't tell.

I found a tube of cherry chapstick at the bottom of my bag and swiped it on.

My own nails were unpainted, bitten to the quick.

When I returned to the store, my friend—could I call the new girl my friend?—was gone. The room was small enough that I could survey it in one glance from the entrance, but still I stepped in, half expecting her to pop up, perhaps from looking at something on a lower rack. When I didn't see her, I walked out to the tiled central hall to wait. I stood straight in the middle of the two-story space, allowing traffic to flow around me like Moses parting the sea.

I watched her walk out of the store a few doors down, an Abercrombie, look right past me, and walk into Claire's. She walked back out after a moment, looking around, and must have decided to walk to the other side, thinking perhaps I had stepped into PacSun (we never went to PacSun). I reached out and touched her arm and she shook it off without even looking.

It wasn't the first time she had failed to find me in a crowd. She told me that her large nose and big eyes made her face distinctive, gave it character. She told me I looked like other people. I had looked at myself for hours, but I didn't see it. Then again, it was so hard to tell what one looked like. I thought I looked like myself, even when I didn't want to.

I ran a few steps to catch up, shouting her name. It hurt my soul to yell.

"My god, I didn't see you," she said. She seemed relieved and maybe a bit irritated. "You were gone for so long."

"I have a headache," I said finally. We were just standing there, in the middle of the hall, still parting the sea together.

Over time, the new girl, who was no longer the new girl, and I drifted apart. As the other girls started to look more and more like her she started to look more and more like them—"You're playing with fire," I warned her, but she didn't listen—until "like them" became, as it so often becomes, "one of them." She just vaporized, dissipated into fumes that no longer smelled like CK One by the way, but like something simpler, sweeter. And what I realized is that I had dodged a bullet—that if she hadn't dissolved into them, I would have dissolved into her, and then who would I be? No, groups were not for me.

~

A year or two later, by which time I had become a runner and she had become just like the others, she was expelled after cheating on the very first test in Ms. Alison's tenth grade geometry class, her answers being identical to those of the girl next to her. And there was a scandal, because it turned out all the girls in the group shared answers, just like they shared everything. They had been copying one another for years, but apparently our grammar school teachers didn't notice or didn't care. In high school, there were some things that couldn't be shared.

She transferred to the public school in her neighborhood where no uniforms were required, as no uniforms were required in any of the suburban public schools in our area.

And when I saw her in the mall again a few years later, she pretended she didn't remember me, or maybe she actually didn't remember me, or maybe she just didn't recognize me, or maybe there isn't really a difference.

~

My parents were surprised that, during a certain phase, I said I wanted to be a casting agent. I could look at a pair of nearly identical looking supermodels and suss out the smallest distinctions. I could tell who was right for New York Fashion Week and who was right for couture and who was right for Guess.

Honestly, I'm still really good at this, and the older I get, the clearer it becomes. I can see through the surface to find the tiniest variations. To this day, I am excellent at telling white girls apart. Too bad there's not much use for it.

~

It has gotten quite late, I realize—my phone says 6pm—and I wonder if I can be seen, crouched as I am on the grass next to a tree, somewhat shielded from the main road by a bush on the right side and a large headstone to the left.

I try to remember when I last peeped the security guards making their rounds, driving slowly in their pickup trucks, peering left and right. It hadn't quite occurred to me then that there was an asymmetry: that I could see them, creeping, but I might not be seen in turn.

I lift up my hands. My skin is very close to the color of the maple bark, especially in shade. I wonder if maybe this was my original purpose: to slip into the wilderness without detection.

If I were naked and pressed myself very closely to the trunk of a tree, I can imagine how I might, from a distance, be difficult to make out.

The cemetery being something like a park, there are squirrels and birds everywhere. Presumably the squirrels rely on senses other than sight to determine whether a solid being is a tree or a human.

Although perhaps such fine distinctions aren't important to squirrels; what matters is dangerous or not dangerous, and I have never been dangerous, not to squirrels, not to anyone.

~

a chameleon, at rest; or

a grasshopper, unlike any grass I've ever seen; or

a fatigued soldier in green and brown fatigues in the depths of Penn Station, strapped with firearms of unknown power, watching as you walk; or

a fawn you might have glimpsed from the highway as you pass, or was it a tree; or

poop, which is the color of mud, which cannot be a coincidence; or

the way that the deeper the hole, the darker and more obscure the color, as if depth and darkness are linked, even though the deeper you go the more you know; or

a pothole, so close to the color of tar that fills it to the brim; or

the way the color of sharp glass is almost the same as the color of glass dulled by waves, but only one draws blood; or

the way nothing on the beach is the color of blood; and

the way that sand resembles cement, and the way that they are nothing like one another; and

the way the sea and the sky converge at the horizon line, no matter where in the world you are; so:

the color of people in the city; the color of tar, the color of smog, the color of stucco, the color of rust, the color of mice, the color of linoleum, the color of broken bottles, the color of hospital walls; my own color.

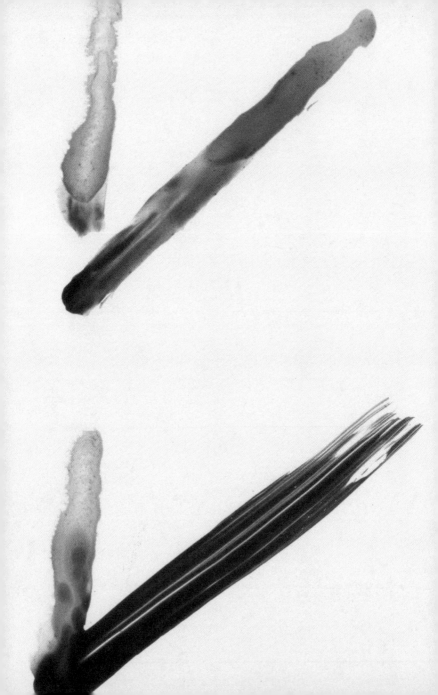

I used to think that time is just one thing, the way a ruler is always the same length, twelve inches or twenty-four inches or even a yard.

Then I started to run and I learned that time is only like distance if we measure distance with taffy or rubber bands or chewing gum or pleats, anything that can expand wide like an accordion or shrink small enough to swallow.

I found that the twenty minutes or thirty minutes of a run could feel like the longest twenty minutes of your life. The final block, the final leg, the final lap, the final half mile—they could feel like the longest hundred feet in the world.

Even when I ran every day, when I felt I could never imagine being more accustomed to something than I was accustomed to running, even then, I sometimes felt I would never reach the end.

There are things you do because they're easy and there are other things you do.

It was an old church, a turn-of-the-century building, each door as big as two or three or even four humans, doors for giants rather than people. So that God can pass through, I guess. I followed the handwritten signs, handed a ten-dollar bill to a bored-looking, bony brunette, took off my shoes, and stepped into the sanctuary. It was enormous; the size of twenty of me on its shortest side and perhaps forty or fifty of me or more on its longest side. The morning sun shone recklessly through the stained glass.

The room was big enough to hold at least a few hundred people, but there were only three of us. And then there were four: the brunette padded into the room wearing several fewer layers than she had in the hall, the beginning of class signaling an opening, as if from chrysalis.

We began with a witnessing practice. Each of us was matched with a partner. The first person closed their eyes and moved however they wanted while the other person watched, in part to monitor our safety and in part to simply be a close observer.

I was matched neither with the instructor nor the brunette, but the fourth, a white woman with solid calves and a flowy top. She began by rolling her head left and then right, then rolling her shoulders and her arms backward and forward. She was graceful, light on her feet, but grounded. She looked like the kind of woman who dances every day. She looked like the kind of person who enjoys a hamburger. There was something thick, solid, reliable about her. I imagine that she is a very good aunt. Her mouth moved slightly as her gestures got bigger. She was finding some momentum in her movements. It was as though she were being tugged lightly left and right, fingers first. She never lost her balance; in fact, she seemed quite content to stay centered. Her toes and ankles and knees and hips were often in a straight line; it was only her torso that swayed a little from left to right.

Where did it come from, I was thinking. How did she know to go left and to go right, to lift her arm up and bring it down? Was she recalling something she had done before? Was she imitating something that was unspooling like a film reel inside her head? Was she responding, however unconsciously, to my presence?

We weren't supposed to touch each other, but we could go all around to look. I tried to keep my own footsteps light as I surrounded her, crouching low to look up, stepping away to get a better view from a distance. The space was huge and only two among the group were dancing, and it didn't seem like she was going to make any sudden movements, so I wasn't worried about her running into anything or getting hurt.

The timer went off. It was my turn. I laid down in the center of the room, my arms above my head stiffly, and wondered what I looked like. I started to roll my body in one direction, a full rotation, and then back in the other direction, a full rotation. I kept going, faster and faster until I felt a touch on my back, which was the signal that I was in danger of hurting myself or someone else. I froze. Was I near a wall, or was I near another person? I felt as though I were at a precipice. I decided to remain still for a moment.

As I lay, I started to think about how much time had passed. The teacher had set a timer for 17.5 minutes, but she was herself dancing, her eyes closed. Perhaps she had gotten the timer wrong. I tried to remember what the woman before me had done. How precious, I was thinking, that those movements were made in the moment and might never happen again. Then again, isn't that all movements? Isn't that all moments? To think of the impossibility of return, and yet the inevitability of our desire—it felt like a spiral, like a helix from my core right into the universe.

When I was a kid, my school organized an annual declamation contest. We chose our texts in English class and performed them in the auditorium in front of a large audience.

As a non-speaker, I declined for medical reasons; no one was about to force me to do it. But in secret, I practiced. I mouthed silently, imagining the voice of Douglass or Sojourner Truth or Maya Angelou bubbling up in my own lungs.

Here's the thing: on tests, my marks were often perfect. I could see sentences in my head as if I were reading straight from the textbook; all I had to do was copy the answers onto the sheets. But now that I was trying to memorize full paragraphs, I came up blank.

I would struggle to remember the first few lines and pretend that I was doing it, sometimes even convince myself that I had done.

I had a record function on the walkman I had kept from childhood and I would make recordings of my secret practices, whispering. And then I would play it back, pacing, looking at the text in one hand, my finger hovering over the play button, frowning. Every word a failure. Every pause a failure.

God, how I tried. It makes me hot even now, knowing how hard I tried.

It seemed that the task was not to remember each bit individually—that might be a thousand individual little memories over the course of a single speech—but rather remembering the place that the words came from, the shape of the sentences, the arc of things, and then somehow the individual words would fit like puzzle pieces, or follow one another like skipping stones.

I needed to find the conditions through which the words could emerge and then wait, allow them to bubble up and over. But all of this was easy to imagine and yet difficult to execute. How could I recreate the conditions of Sojourner Truth or Frederick Douglass or JFK or Maya Angelou, me, with my four walls made of sheet-rock, with my pale paint and wallpaper border, with my white metal bed and Formica desk?

One day, I read about "memory palaces" and it clicked. My room was a court; my house was my kingdom.

A Rock—this was the step in front of my door

A River—this was the glass half-moon embedded in the door itself, glass being clear as a river

A Tree — this was the door itself, being made of wood, which was of course made of trees

Hosts—this was me, opening and beckoning, although in real life I never answered the door, I barely even went downstairs

to species—and now I looked down at my lumpy feet, my hardened teenage body

long—because my spine lengthened as I looked

since—because it prickled as I bent, I sensed

departed—and now I was trying to shuffle, head first

Mark—"And he looked up, and said, I see men as trees, walking." Chapter 8, verse 24.

the mastodon—by now I was fully bent, half mast, chewing

The dinosaur—my tongue like a reptile chews its cud

who—and grunts and coos at its neighbor
left—as it departs this earth
dry—desiccated and blown
tokens—worthless, pennies
of their sojourn here—ain't I?
on our planet —on this plane, flat
floor—oak
Any broad alarm—and so it continued, all the way
through to *Good morning*.

How long had it been? I sneaked my eyes open and was
startled to see that my witness wasn't watching me at
all; she was gazing, enraptured, at the instructor, who
was performing some acrobatic sequence of movements
with energy and intensity. Like some graceful bird, with
skimming and hopping and flight. Me, I was still lying,
stiffened, on the edge of the room, unexpectedly alone.
Freer for being unseen. Or was I?

After we debriefed—my partner reddened when I
told her I wasn't mad she had betrayed me, and then
said indignantly that my stillness itself had been the first
betrayal, and that my choice to open my eyes was the
second and more unforgivable—after all of that, the
teacher taught us a lesson.

She believed that the hip flexors, and particularly the
iliopsoas muscles, which run from the thigh to the core,
are responsible for everything that was wrong with us,

muscular and bony and even psychological and spiritual. *And my shins?* I asked. *Even your shins,* she told me.

We could loosen, she said, by following a specific sequence of movements.

She moved her arm one way and I followed.

She rolled onto her back and I followed that too.

Her leg lifted and curled behind her.

There were no mirrors in this room. Am I doing it right, I asked her? She told me to focus on how I felt, not how I looked.

She grabbed one toe with the "peace fingers" of the other hand. I tried to do the same thing.

She told me to relax, and then looked at me and said it again, and I resented her. I was relaxed. I was relaxed. I was sending energy, like she told me to do, to the front of my pelvis and the back of my calf. I felt myself beginning to sink. I was fighting, but it felt like balancing.

Stop gripping, she said, and I unwound. She put her hand on my shoulder—*Stop gripping*—and I unwound a little more. She moved a hand under my shoulder—*Into my hand,* she said, and I softened. She touched the other shoulder and I sank. She put her hand between the blades and I felt as though I were releasing into a pillow. She put her hand under my knee and it flattened, and with it my hip finally released, and I thought in wonder *this is what they mean when they say all the way,* and I had never felt more open, and I let a little sigh escape from my chest like a tiny, tiny roar.

"Good morning."

~

I must have drifted off, because when I opened my eyes, the room was empty and I felt the absence of the instructor's healing hands like a hole. I was extremely alert. I could hear cars from the intersection two blocks down, and birds from just outside the window, and the murmur of footsteps downstairs. My being was deeply attuned to the universe, shifting like a knob from one frequency to the next.

I made my way to my feet, blood rushing to my head. My socks and shoes were in the hallway where I had left them. The brunette who had taken my money was sitting where she had been sitting before class began. The instructor was nowhere to be found.

I looked again at the brunette. She appeared just as she had two hours ago: phone in hand, vacant. How did I lose time, the way other people lose their keys?

I hated leaving. It felt as though walking out the door was reversing my steps, as though everything that had just happened would be undone bit by bit, so that by the time I arrived home and took off my clothes and laid down in bed, I would be as I had been, lying down in bed that morning. As though nothing even happened at all.

~

In college, they called it retrograde: the art of winding and unwinding yourself like one of those spinners people put in their yards, those swirly things that turn and then turn back, no allegiance at all, whatever direction the wind blows, they go.

We were meant to learn every exercise on our right side, and then on our left. We practiced the same material, stationary and on the diagonal. We learned with our faces to the mirror and with the mirror at our backs. Every little thing taught on the left, then on the right. Every long line going forward, then in reverse.

In the end, it was the retrograde that did me in, how I was supposed to bounce like a witch from the ground to my knees, to float like a fairy from my knees to my toes. I was weighed down, even as a college student with barely a care in the world, too heavy to fly the way we were supposed to fly.

As though every individual joint was filled not with air or fluid but density. Every bone having its own center of gravity that pulled me toward the ground.

As though my body only wanted to move down and my mind only wanted to move forward.

It's why I gave up dance and went back to running. I could only ever go one way.

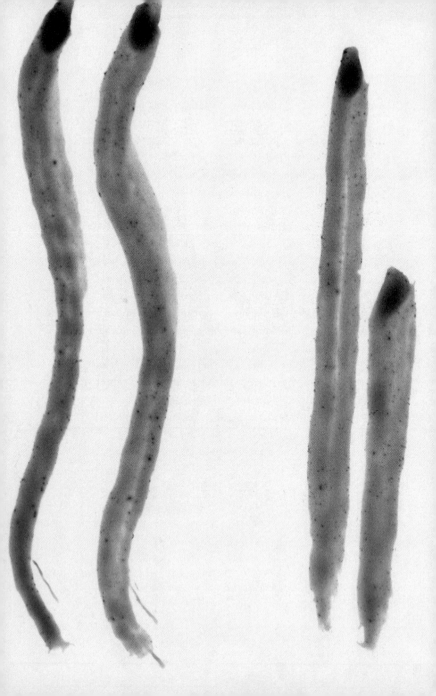

Will I ever run again, though, is really the question I return to again and again like a hurt tooth. Will I ever run again? I think it obsessively, repeatedly.

On some level, of course I will run.

I will, for example, suddenly hear the subway arriving and spring down the stairs, sprint through the station into the open doors.

I will notice that the walk sign is rapidly counting down and will jog to the other side of the street, too impatient to wait.

I will jog a few steps to catch up with a friend.

I will run. But will I run?

Sometimes I shift from questions to declarations—I will never run again, period, full stop—and I am filled with despair.

I say despair as though it were a bad thing, but the truth is that I savor it a bit, the way you savor the pain of a breakup.

To no longer want to run would be to forget how beautifully it hurt, running. I wasn't ready to forget that feeling.

It's funny, the way pain dampens your desire to do anything.

And at the same time, the way pain is really the only gas you have to put in the tank. They say "running on fumes" as if it were a problem, like fumes aren't the best part. It's the fumes that get you high.

I woke up before my six o'clock alarm, adrift and anxious.

My shins felt fresh, as they always do in the morning when I'm lying down.

Since my diagnosis, I had been dragging throw pillows from the couch to elevate my legs as I slept, thinking it might increase the blood flow.

Every morning, I wonder if I have healed overnight.

Every morning, I am afraid to get out of bed, afraid that as soon as my feet touch the ground, it will hurt.

I had forgotten to ask the doctor how bone grows together, if there will always be a seam.

Once a week, I got an email from my neighborhood app. The neighborhood, like so many in New York, was really two neighborhoods, one old and one new laid right on top of one another, a boulder as big as a person placed carefully over something thin and delicate, like a tulip. That feeling of crushing.

The reports included development updates ("the empty lot is turning into a condo building, I hope they don't take away all of our parking") and practical questions ("what do y'all think of the watermelons sold by the watermelon man who parks on Atlantic?"). Mostly they spied on each other, posted photos from their doorbell cams, asked questions about the new "mailman," posted reports about the people who were rifling through their recycling for bottles to return, and so on.

I liked to know what was going on around town. I liked to read the classifieds, in particular, in case something appealed to me. Maybe it was time to buy a car. Maybe somebody was giving away a house plant.

I was skimming reports about community board meetings and recent thefts and lost puppies and requests for roofers, and then I stopped, my heartbeat rising.

It was a link to an article from the local rag. "Brooklyn resident honored in ceremony," it said, describing her accomplishments as a social worker and her involvement with a neighborhood association not far from my own apartment.

There were two photographs. The first showed a woman of indeterminate age, perhaps 30, perhaps 40, perhaps even 50, surrounded by family in front of a yellow house with white trim. Did I recognize the house? I looked at it closely. I didn't think so, but it wouldn't be hard to find.

I inspected the second image carefully, zoomed in to see the details. The head shot was golden and warm, but her expression was defiant. She had sepia skin and a modest cap of curls that surrounded her head like a halo. The picture reminded me a bit, actually, of those images from the '80s of the Black astronaut Bessie Jemison, her hair mirroring the shape of her helmet, except this woman wasn't smiling. She was small, tight, like me.

It was pouring rain. I grabbed my umbrella and a handful of Advil and began to walk south.

I headed to the woman's street and walked carefully from the northern end to the southern terminus, glancing at each building along the way, looking for yellow with white trim. It was a quiet collection of blocks, full of families who had lived there for a generation or more and took care of their properties even if the city didn't take care of them.

When I didn't see it, I zigged right and then left at the stop signs, doubling back and going around the block.

Later it would occur to me that a dog, or some other alibi, might be helpful on days like this, when I'm not running. Something that can serve as its own explanation.

On my fourth try, a little one-block street off the main avenue, I found myself soaking wet, ten feet from the woman herself, standing still in the doorsill, shielded from the rain by a tiny little shade that extended over the entry.

Water was somehow entering my galoshes, and my raincoat was not so much waterproof as shrugging at water, raising an eyebrow at it before ushering it in. I had never minded a bit of weather inside the house, metaphorically speaking, but I knew most others were not like me.

The little eyebrow over the front door shouldn't have been enough shelter, but it was. She was wearing a giant muumuu and discreet plastic glasses. Functional rubber clogs, although she was clearly hoping to avoid taking another step. Surprisingly muscled, slender legs—I always notice the legs. A little dog yipped through her yard, racing at me, then circling back to her, then running back toward me, on high alert.

She didn't move, as if she were used to this kind of drama. In fact, she was so still, I would have thought she was indeed a statue—a mannequin, or a scarecrow, or a Santa, or whatever life-sized statues people have in Brooklyn—except she was leaning against the doorsill in a way that statues don't usually lean.

"Good afternoon," I finally said, as if that were an excuse. It sounded forced, even to my own ears.

"Good afternoon," she told me, her voice lilting downward. Unlike me, she sounded like a woman who was used to being listened to. Like a woman with a job. Possibly like a woman with children. It was a voice that was good at nipping protests in the bud.

A drop of water slid from the roof onto her hand. She recoiled as if she had been singed.

~

As I stood, looking at the woman, I was reminded of something that happened just a few days ago.

There are benches in the park, dotted with families eating ice cream and people on angry one-sided conversations with their headsets, or women taking photos of their own selves, or white people taking self-satisfied portraits of the diversity that surrounds them.

When I'm in the park, I'm often running, or at least walking. I rarely have a reason to stop.

But that day, there was something in my shoe and instead of lifting my leg to remove it, lunging against a fire hydrant or bike rack, I decided to sit on the relatively clean and nearly empty bench in front of me, I shuffled some leaves aside and made sure to stay near the corner, vaguely aware of a form at the other end.

Of course, once I stopped, I felt a sense of physical relief as well as anxiety to be off my feet—I had been going for nearly two hours, I realized. I looked around.

This was the busiest part of the park, close to the YMCA, at the crossroads of the basketball courts and the tennis courts and the baseball fields. On the street, someone was playing loud music while washing their car.

To my right, a small child was half running, half balancing, legs splayed on either side of a bike, tiptoes barely grazing the ground so that he had to run at a little lean and careen from one foot to the next. His older brother or friend, the bigger kid in front of him, was reluctantly and with a sense of actual, lifelong resignation waiting, riding and waiting, as though he had only ever been waiting and expected to hold back or be held back his entire life. The littler one, a few steps behind, seemed equally resigned, as if aware that the future was equally bleak with his brother or without him.

The boys circled back and I realized they were headed to my very bench. Six or seven feet away, on the other side of several armrest barriers, was a woman who must have been their mother. She was wearing a surprisingly sensible t-shirt and jeans, sandals, a baseball cap, and looked to be in her late thirties or early forties. Her haircut was also sensible, but a bit frazzled, as if she were a professional woman who kept it together during the week but didn't have time to worry about the weekends. She was holding an iPad and a dark tote with colored trim, out of which I could see a legal pad and a pile of books. She had one eye on the boys and one eye on the iPad, and without looking up she produced two cans with her left hand and a bag of chips with her right.

"Can we get some ice cream," the older boy said without wheedling, working on his can—it wasn't really a question—

She responded in the same matter-of-fact tone, "Nope." He looked up for a second. "There's ice cream at the house" she added.

"We're not at the house," he muttered into the can as he walked away.

I was looking at her, at the way she presented such a controlled and all-encompassing feeling of competence, and wondered if you had to be a mother to learn it. How competent was I, or how competent did I appear?

I took a neutral audit of myself, in relation to this woman. I was wearing a black tank top and leggings, a tote, a baseball cap. I had no chips. I had a moleskin and not a legal pad. I had no children. I had no iPad. I had no "I could take you or leave you" kind of attitude that the best mothers always bring to their children, who therefore know exactly where they stand at all times. In fact, although I felt relatively calm, I probably appeared quite anxious. My nails were ragged, half-bitten. My hair had not been combed in days. I clearly did not have a regular job. It was after sunset but I had not removed my sunglasses, as though I had something to hide, which maybe I did.

I leaned forward slightly to match the other woman's stance, crossed my right leg over my left like hers. I started concentrating very hard on the angle of my neck and found that if I focused on the exposed part of my throat, on making it convex rather than concave, I could brace my inside while still breathing normally. The bracing helped me stay still.

It was a trick I had learned in a class I had taken in Canada a few years before. I had turned myself into a statue and my classmates had dragged me around. I remember closing my eyes and feeling the back of my heels get hot with the friction. I imagined my feet like brooms, picking up the dust and earth that were in that room, that had been left behind by the people before. At first we were moved by groups of four people, and then three people, then two, then only one. The last person who moved me got quite close. He had put his arms in the seam between my biceps and my breasts and held them stiff in front, like a toy solder, and when he straightened his legs my whole body came off the ground, and then he carried me like that, to the other side of the room, and I stayed stiff, stiff as a plank, every muscle hardened and stony, until we reached the other side. He *pliéed* gently to bring my feet back to the ground but when he withdrew his arms, I toppled to the side like a lamp. It was in that feeling of suspension right before I fell, when I realized that I could not activate the muscles I needed to stand without softening and I wasn't ready to be soft.

My skin is quite brown and I rarely see bruises. But the marks on my left side were visible from certain angles for weeks, as if my thigh and hip and shoulder and forearm had been painted with a long brush. I think it was the stiffness of my neck and throat that saved me from more serious injury.

As I have often found that stiffness can save one from serious injury.

And so, I find myself defaulting to stiffness in times of need.

I do not know if I needed to become a statue in order to imagine myself as the mother next to me, but it helped. Do I need to imagine myself as the mother next to me? What if "stiff" is the opposite of "mother"? Is that why there aren't more statues of mothers?

I stayed still in that position for some minutes or hours after the family had gone, the mother sending me one last look of confusion, the young boy following the older boy following the mother like chicks following and having imprinted on a duck or a goose or a chicken. I could see them out of the corner of my eye and I wanted to get in line too, but I did not.

I don't know how long I was on the sidewalk, "good afternoon"-ing. It might not have been more than a few milliseconds. I don't know that my legs ever stopped moving.

I remember walking—I like the feeling of a wet face, so ambiguous—to the end of the block, and up and down some nearby streets, until I got tired of sloshing around in my shoes and headed home, shrugging my shoulders and releasing.

～

Was the woman the "someone else" the man from the subway thought I might be? Like me, but a future version of me. The possibility made me shiver.

On second thought—there is always a second thought and so often it is the reverse of the first—this stranger didn't resemble me at all.

～

I was less than a mile away from the grocery store and decided to stop by, caress my boy Antwaun's peeling face, maybe take a quick walk through the aisles for old time's sake. The supermarket would be good shelter from the dampness in the air.

My eyes were on the sidewalk as I recreated the steps of my previous walk, jumping over the cracks just as I had done before, though of course there was no record and it might not have been "just," if just is "exactly." But if just is "nearly" or "a just person would judge this as similar," I think I might meet that standard. I tried to match the feeling if not the exact image. I wasn't paying as much attention as I could, and I hopped right past Antwaun's resting place. I was all the way at the next block before I realized I had passed him. And then turned around to see that I had missed the spot, but I had not missed Antwaun: he was simply gone, painted over with thick white rolled strokes, as if he had never existed at all.

Whereas Antwaun had previously occupied a corner, now the entire wall was covered with white paint. On the right, a pile of black lines didn't look like a person yet, but rather something like a map or a flower. When I squinted, they coalesced into a cluster that vaguely resembled Barack Obama's head. As I got closer, I saw a sign indicating the name of an artist and a city agency. I couldn't believe it was legal, to erase a person like this.

~

"It was never official," she said, slowly putting my juice into a giant grocery bag. "So they had to replace it with something official." The upper half of her face burst: her eyes welled up under her false lashes, and her blue contacts looked glassy and distant. Her nose and mouth, though, kept the same grim expression.

"It was official to me," I said. "It looked good." I took the bag.

"It was a real good picture of Antwaun," she said, resting her manicure against the black rubber of the conveyor belt. "I said to my sister it looked just like him."

I waited for her to go on. "I liked seeing it there, when I came in. I felt like he was watching me, but not in a weird way, not like no ghost, just like…" She glanced behind me to the aisle, as if for the words she couldn't bring herself to say, or perhaps for a reprieve, but the store was almost empty.

"Like?" I barely breathed it.

"Like if he were still here," she said. "Like knowing somebody familiar in the room even if they're not right there with you, you know what I mean? Like somebody you know in the building. Like knowing you're watched, but in a good way, you know what I mean?

Like somebody's looking over your shoulder, but in a good way, you know what I mean? Like … like somebody's watching, that's the only way I can describe it. Like I got … not shivers, but just like, this warm feeling because I knew he was there. You know what I'm saying? Like … like when you pray, you know what I mean? Like God."

I knew exactly what she meant.

~

"He was never really there," I wanted to say. "I mean, not really." But I knew that wouldn't make her feel better.

"I mean, he's always there," I wanted to say, "I mean he's always here," but I knew that wasn't quite right either.

~

I thought about the fine, rubbery bits of red and white I had carried last week or whenever it was, sheltered between my nails and the pads of my fingers. Were they all that was left? Had they crumbled into dust? "I miss him too," is what I actually said, and I had never met him but it was true, it was true.

~

I found myself making excuses to walk in the general direction of the woman's house, not because I wanted to run into her, but because I wanted to find out what would happen if she ran into me. You know what they say: everything you touch touches you.

~

Do you ever think about how good it would feel to do Double Dutch? To skip and keep skipping. To always be facing. To be caught in those ropes.

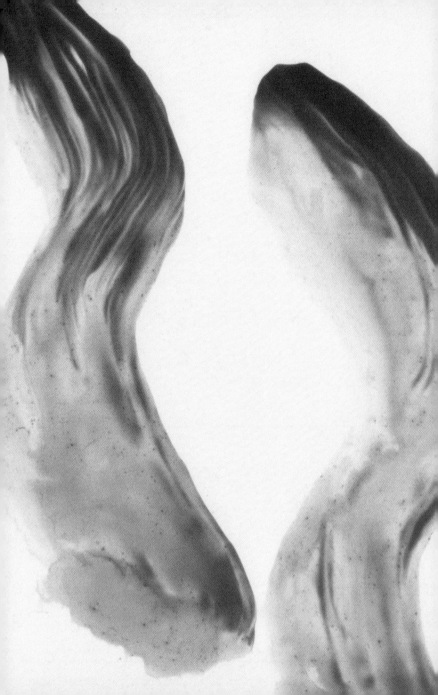

The border between outside and inside the store was almost invisible, a gossamer thread of light and nearly imperceptible wave of anti-theft electric shields. But there was no mistaking the transfiguration that unfolded when you passed through: everything a bit bluer, a bit cooler, a bit cleaner.

As I pulled open the glass door, a cluster of teenagers shoved past, tight as a stem of grapes, so many heads in a mass and a single voice as if springing from a single sprig.

The place must contain thousands of t-shirts, compressed back-to-back-to-back into a metal rack. I imagined unfolding the hangers like an accordion, top after top after

top after top after top

On television, police often find the DNA of a third party on the victim's clothing, like a sweater or a sock. That used to be enough to incriminate you. If your DNA was found, you were caught, done.

These days, the instruments are so sensitive, maybe too sensitive. Any little flake, any little drop, they can read it like a book. The problem is that everybody is shedding all the time. Those little bits could be the careless traces of a perpetrator, but they truly could have been deposited by anyone whose skin passed over the clothes before they arrived at their destination, a garment factory worker or retail employee or even a regular person who tried it on, but it didn't fit.

I suppose that's why they tell you to wash your clothes before you wear them, so you can be sure in the case of an accident that the slate, so to speak, is truly clean.

I'd better hope that none of the people who buy these shirts are murdered, I thought as I rubbed the fuzzy sweater in one aisle, the silky camisole in another, wondering what traces might be on my hands besides me. I thought of the gaggle of girls at the entrance. They were the only people I had touched today.

I was usually a pants person—you never know when you'll want or need to run—but I had come here today looking for something else. I was thinking that maybe my legs would benefit—psychically (do my shins have a psyche? they certainly seem to have a mind of their own) or molecularly, or in some other invisible way—from more oxygen.

As I tried and tried and tried things on, I could overhear a woman talking to her own mother. "Is it too tight?" "I don't think so." "Look, I can get two fingers here inside the waist. I can get a whole fist in here." "Should I get another size?" "I don't like seeing my ankles." "I think they're supposed to be baggy." "I think they're supposed to be tight." "See, it says 'loose fit.'" "It says 'boyfriend fit.'" "My boyfriend's leg is the width of my arm." "It says 'mom fit.'" "These say 'dad' fit." "Who borrows clothes from their dad?" "I wear your dad's shirts all the time." "This makes my neck look small." "Your neck *is* small." "I'm like a bobble head." "Unbutton it more." "What do you think?" "What do you think?"

The mirror was slightly tilted to elongate my body, yes, but also my face, so that I looked like a slightly more oval version of myself. I started by taking off my shirt and putting on another. I slid it off and tried a larger size. It was perfect. Then I tried a size that was even bigger. Also perfect. But how? I switched between the two for a while, unable to decide which was right. I pulled on a skirt over my own joggers, which I was still wearing. I added a cardigan. I pulled off the pants and left the skirt. I added a scarf.

I examined myself in the mirror. From the outside, I was entirely intact. My skin sparkled, the light coat of Vaseline I applied after my shower covering me like a shield. The skirt draped just below my knees. It didn't look bad with my tennis shoes. You would never be able to tell, looking at them from the outside, that there was anything wrong.

When I opened the door to get a better view in the hallway trifold, I realized that the one I had thought was the mother was the daughter, her voice corporate and deep, and the one I had thought was the daughter was the mother, her voice thin and gravelly.

It was the mother who was staring at the mirror, shifting first one foot forward then the other. Her lips were thin, her skin sallow and powdery, her makeup afternoon-settled into the folds of her face. The jumpsuit did not flatter her. Our gazes crossed; she seemed startled to have been diverted from her own reflection. "I'm not a good person to ask," she said finally, although I hadn't asked anything at all. "I never wear brown. It—it washes me out."

I retreated to my stall, shuffling like a horse.

I was back at the mall the next day, and many more days after that. I meandered in that direction on my walks. Sometimes I stopped by before or after trips to the city. Sometimes I went there for dinner. It was an unexpected rediscovery—I thought I moved to the city to get away from malls, and here I am, decades later, finding that I actually like them just as much as I remembered from childhood. The parts I had disliked—the sense that someone was always watching me, in those double-height atriums, the sense that everyone I knew was converging in one building and walking around and around it like a roller-skating rink—those parts didn't follow into the city version. But the parts I liked—the choices and yet the sameness—never failed to deliver.

I liked the people who came to the mall. They were the kind of people who wanted to be able to find the same shape in different sizes, the same fabric in different colors. They got cookies at the Baskin-Robbins on the second floor and drank appletinis at TGI Fridays, where you didn't have to take off your baseball cap to sit down, where you could enjoy yourself in public, knowing that everyone on both floors could see you smile, where you could feel confident that your bodysuit and matching heels and matching nails and matching dye job would be seen and appreciated in the full view of warm fluorescent lights.

And then there was my store. Each small shift in inventory was a delight. Same top, now with sleeves. Same cardigan, but in the stretchy material of last week's sweats. I even liked looking at the underwear, bundled in plastic packages of three, always one size or another running out. They call the fashion "fast," but in many ways it felt reassuringly incremental to me, the way slight variations opened and unfolded week after week, as though I were watching foliage shift, one leaf, one bloom, forever.

You could only bring eight garments into the dressing room at a time. I got used to dropping an armful at the threshold, telling the watchful worker "eleven," "twenty," "fourteen." No matter what I said, no matter how friendly (ha!) and trustworthy I tried to appear, she would count the hangers one by one.

Since my diagnosis, I dreaded getting dressed. Now that I couldn't run, I showered less frequently. I would often wear the same thing for days at a time. In the gauzy light of the dressing room, everything felt soft and smooth. But at home, all the fabrics felt scratchy, even after washing. The putting things on was the worst part. Everything felt thick around my neck as I pulled it over my head, tense around my hips, dense around my thighs. Only after a few days—I would sleep in my clothes and continue to wear them upon waking—did I find peace.

~

I remember, as a child, receiving a set of paper dolls. Funny how they're called *dolls* when they crumpled and crunched under my thick fingers as a kid. Being more like a shadow than a doll, really.

I must have been seven or eight, old enough to use scissors without stabbing myself.

I gave them names and occupations but really, they were so disappointingly flat.

I'm pretty sure I burned the dolls in a candle or on the stove or—now I remember—on a halogen lamp. I watched the paper darken and singe for a moment, then let it float to the couch, where it sizzled before quickly dying away. I was old enough to scold, maybe seven or eight. My mother, pragmatic, turned the pillow so that the scorch couldn't be seen, but I knew it was there. I would sneak over and finger it when no one was looking, the way you press a bruise or wiggle a tooth.

The insides of the couch were surprisingly yellow, the color of urine, which at the time was one of the

colors (golden) and textures (molten liquid) I considered
a possibility for my own inner core. I had seen diagrams
of the Earth's crust in school, brown on the outer layer
and a ball of fire in the middle. Even my skin had a
slightly yellowish tint, I had noticed, which seemed like
a signal. Still, though I was soft and the couch was
soft, it was hard to imagine that we were made of the
same stuff.

It became my favorite game, to pretend the cushion
hated being squished flat by my father and loved being
cuddled softly by me, and bemoaned the burn, her scar,
and wanted surgery. I was so sorry I had hurt her. If I
could have made her whole I would have. My mother
frowned when she saw me patting and stroking, but she
said nothing.

One day I came home from class and saw that the
shape of the couch was the same, with the same fabric,
but new. No burn. No marks. No wear. I was more dis-
tressed by the fact that the fabric was the same than I
would have been had the entire couch been replaced,
I think. Imagine being replaced with improved,
less flawed, more perfect skin stretched around the
same shape.

As I examined the new couch, I realized it had zip-
pers around the cushions. I didn't need to burn anything
to see inside; I could just slide off the case. Underneath
was the original fabric, so that the inner layer was the
same as the outer layer, which covered it like an extra
layer of bark covers an inner layer of bark.

I loved unzipping the sleeve and watching them slide, one past the other, so that my inner cushion could breathe. That outer cover and inner layer were, come to think of it, something like a paper doll, folding.

Those dolls: I remember exactly when I thought of them last. In college, I worked as a typist for a philosopher, a former graduate student at my university who had taught there briefly in the '70s.

She didn't have a computer; the arthritis in her hands prevented her from typing. She had developed a method of scrawling with a pencil onto loose-leaf, fisting a pencil tightly, and making elegant little loops and lines on paper in continuous cursive streams, the end of each line connected with a long zig to the beginning of the next. I never learned to read her shorthand, but she referred to it during our sessions. She would speak continuously and carefully for an hour, our coffee getting cold as I tapped, for about two thousand words each session, then ask me to read back what she had dictated and I had written.

What was the book about? It's hard to say. She was interested in physical habits and intuitions, and the tools we use to refine them. Her research began during her teenage years. She had grown up in Brooklyn and had studied first at a magnet school for the arts, and later at Brown University, which had just begun to accept women. As a student, she had initially intended to work specifically at the intersection of anthropology and dance, as Katherine Dunham had done, but in her second year things began to change.

"I had been working so hard," she always spoke slowly for my benefit, although I was quite a fast typist, "on my second-year performance, called *The Pomegranate Seed*, in which I myself inhabited the figure of the seed and was constantly being enveloped, being buried in arid land, piercing and growing. I was trying to use language from my own childhood in order to reinterpret the masters, you see. Although of course we rejected language like 'masters' during those days." She laughed, almost a cackle.

And so the problem became, she continued, how to develop a language of self-control without using the vocabulary of master and slave. It was a theoretical question and also a philosophical question with important implications for the ways we understood and managed our own bodies. Whose bodies were they, anyway? Were they ours? Could a body be one's own possession?

My work with the philosopher changed me permanently, attracted me to certain things and repelled me from others, established certain habits of speech, even changed the way I hold my head. I actually don't remember most of the book—which was a kind of endless memoir of her own youth—but this story, in particular, I have never forgotten.

I began to wonder, the philosopher said, *whether my body belonged to me at all, or whether it might not in fact be part of a collective. The idea was not my own, but was gifted to me by Huey P. Newton; I had traveled to Boston to see him speak of communalism and revolutionary enthusiasm during my first year of college, and it made quite an impression. You see, my relationship to classical dance had involved a corps; the beauty of it was getting lost in the group. Yes, there was something uniquely attractive about groups. And this was how I became interested in attraction. My question was this: how was it that I got stuck to others, as part of a flock?*

I took a biology class and began to wonder whether there wasn't in fact something chemical about it. After all, atoms, molecules, are made up of little… pieces, let's say… that are energetically connected to one another, sometimes temporarily, sometimes nearly permanently, although of course those bonds can always dissipate or be violently severed—I learned that too.

I started to think about my own body as something temporary, something that had arrived, had its day, and would dissipate as well. I also started to think about my body in dialogue with others. Me and my partner and my neighbor, weren't we all made out of the same… kinds of atoms? The same little bits? The same stuff?

And then I gave this performance about pomegranate seeds for a special event put on by the theater club. I still remember the rehearsal studio where I came up with the piece. It was sunny with dusty wood floors that I had to clean carefully before I began. Of course, I couldn't escape the footsteps of the dancers that had come before me, those invisible palimpsests on the floor of the studio. Those little marks were exactly the point. The challenge was how to find them. I somehow knew that erasing the new would get me closer to the old, and it felt important to start fresh, sweeping and mopping before I even tried to begin. These days I never sweep, as I'm sure you've noticed—I say that as an aside, no need to include it in your document.

Indeed, our typing sessions often took place in her home, and it's true that the dust would accumulate for weeks before the housecleaner arrived. The cleaner was a grim, muscular woman who vanquished the grime as if—this is what I used to think—as if the dust were her husband's mistress or some other similar, personal, enemy. The philosopher liked to have the windows open, and the dirt always came back.

But when I was a student, the ritual of cleaning was quite important to me. I couldn't see the ones who had come before, but I could feel them. I would walk slowly around the studio, eyes peeled, staring at the floor, all of my receptors vibrating, listening for a clue. I thought if I could excavate—energetically, I suppose—the history of this dance floor, I might be able to tap into something they had left for me, maybe make something new out of it.

I began to go to the room late at night, with a candle—we weren't meant to be working overnight, but I had learned how to rig the door when I left so that it only appeared to be locked—to wait for the spirits to show up. I became convinced this was the only legitimate way to build a practice. There was no creation, there was only listening. There was no invention, there was only re-connection. I didn't know where to look except for the ancestors.

It sounds... it sounds... I suppose it sounds mystical. But it's true. It is the only place to look.

At any rate, over time I came to recognize the problem with my method. There were several problems, in fact. One was the uncertainty that came with all of this listening. Even when I was sure I was tuning into something important, it was never totally clear whether I was properly channeling it or whether I was putting too much of my own self into it, too much invention. At the very least, I may have been choosing what to hear and ignoring other voices, consciously or unconsciously, and that knowledge was very uncomfortable to me, a significant challenge to my method.

Another problem was the problem of interference. Any method that could only be accomplished surreptitiously in the dead of night felt wrong, and try as I might, I couldn't really connect with the ancestors during the day, when other girls were running around in the halls and people were honking and teaching. Yet I was suspicious of any practice that was only available at special times and in particular ways.

And then, I was also worried about being right. How did I know that what I heard was being interpreted correctly? I would draft my ideas and perform them at night with my candle. I would wait for a response. But it was like waiting for a Ouija board, honestly. Everything was always just a little hazy, and what I really wanted—the whole point, really, of developing such a rigorous practice—was clarity.

I performed the pomegranate seed choreography at a happening that featured, among other things, a talking dance in which someone yelled "No" six hundred and sixty-six times—you wouldn't believe how quickly some people can yell—and a very beautiful balletic pas de deux featuring a dancer who had been, I heard, an apprentice at the New York City Ballet.

I don't think there's much to say about my own work that night except that it was based on what I heard, transcribed, and tried my best to learn, however imperfectly, whatever my misgivings. The performance involved opening and closing my body, as if I were being opened and closed with two thumbs.

Afterward, I was taking off my knee pads and my wristbands—I always had to wear knee pads in those days; I looked more like a football player than a ballerina—and a young brother came up to me.

"That was lovely," he told me. He had thin, shapely eyes and skin the color of a chickpea. I rolled my eyes as I pulled on my slippers. "No really," he continued. And I remember exactly what he said after that. He said, "At least it was about something." I remember it because I was so offended in that moment. Like, what did he expect. About something. Of course it was.

I turned to him like "Is that supposed to be a compliment?" and began to walk away, my knapsack slung over my shoulder.

He followed me, protesting, "That's not what I meant at all," he said. "I mean listen, I'm twenty years old, and I bet you—I mean—what I mean to say is, for me, 'at least' is as good as I've got. For now. 'At least' is a good start." I kept walking, but I understood what he meant and I got a little softer. He continued: "I mean, I am trying to figure it out. Like, what are the limits of metaphor? Are our bodies already seeds, getting ready to grow something?" I glanced back and swear I saw him blush a little, but he carried on, "and, well, why do we bother trying to represent anything anyway?"

"The real challenge," he continued, is "excess effort."

I stopped, truly embarrassed now. "Excess?" In my world, there was nothing so shameful as trying too hard.

"Yes—I mean—not excess as in 'too much' as in 'doesn't look good'," he blushed again, "but 'excess' as in 'more than the body requires for expression'."

"Tell me more."

"I'm talking about finding ease. How can we make the body feel easy? How do we build a meaningful relationship to… things?"

Yes. This was exactly it.

"I play cello," he continued. "—or, I did play cello, growing up. Now I'm not sure. I want to get into improvisation, but I've found that everything I play sounds the same. It sounds like me. I want to learn how to sound like something else. I want to reflect or represent something else or someone else. And as I was watching your performance, I was thinking about whether you were really reflecting the pomegranate seed, or is it you that I see unfolding? Like when you did that thing with your hand. I was thinking, is this a move she's done before? Is this part of her…repertoire, her vocabulary, so to speak? Or is it something new, something invented in order to represent this specific object, this seed? Can you use the same tools to represent different things? I mean, in some ways the answer to that question is obvious. Of course you can. You can because you're doing the work in the same body. But you are also trying to point to something different? What are the possibilities of that pointing? How far can it go?"

We had arrived at an intersection near my apartment. I was buzzing, tense from the adrenaline of the performance, barely registering what he was saying but also, somehow, listening with

heightened receptivity (are bees receptive? are their bodies soft?).
Part of me wanted to listen to this guy talk, but part of me wanted
to go to my room and sit quietly and listen to music and think about
what had just happened to me. I paused.

"I mean, listen," he said, "have you ever thought about the
way your head balances on your body?"

"I'm a dancer," I told him. "Of course I have. It's all I think
about."

"Yes, but——" I watched him stumble. "I mean the tension in
your neck. I mean, your inhibitions, and how they're tied to your
head? I mean, your shoulders are lifted right now. Are you sure
you're not tense? Are you holding something in? I mean——"

I interrupted him. "I'm tired."

"Oh, of course…"

"And I'm interested in what you're saying about cello and
symbols and pointing. But now is not the time."

"Yes, yes, okay," he said. "Um, do you want to talk sometime?
Maybe later this week?"

"Sure. How about tomorrow?" I was feeling bold. And why
not? Here was someone who promised to hold the clues I was
looking for. It felt very urgent to talk, just not right then. We made
plans to meet the next evening at nine.

There was a bar in the lower level of one of the Gothic build-
ings on campus. I remember that it was hidden amidst classrooms
and faculty offices, right next to one of the minor libraries, and
that it was dim but never entirely dark—as though the university
was keeping an eye on you. My friend was waiting when I arrived,
sunken into a giant brown couch, probably gifted by some rich
alumna's interior decorator when they redid the house on the Cape.

Maybe it was the scale of the couch or the tiny tumbler of scotch in his hand, but he seemed smaller than I remembered.

"I'm here," I announced, folding one leg beneath me as I put down my things. I was always surrounded by bags. One bag had leg warmers, knee pads, chalk, extra socks; another bag had raw almonds, dried apricots, cough drops, a flask with water; another one had books, notebooks, reference images; another had makeup, tissues.

I smoked in those days—everybody did—and he was quick with the match when I pulled out my cigarette.

"Yes you are," he agreed. A half smile was the most I ever saw from him. At least I didn't have to wonder if he was laughing at me.

I looked around. Dregs.

"Have you read The Symposium?" He asked.

"I have not."

"It's a conversation about love," he began. And that's where it started.

Fast forward to two months later, when we finished stitching. The bind, as we liked to call it, attached us back to back.

We could walk by shifting side to side. We had to go every-where together. Our friends could only talk to one of us at a time. Sex—with each other, had we wanted to, or with anyone else for that matter—was entirely impossible. We could not sit, but we could lean.

People understood that this was not us, this was a "project." But they also assumed we were sleeping together, even though there was nothing sexual in it. In fact, the entire performance was a kind of extended audition for summer study he hoped to undertake in

Paris, presumably without me. Having been introduced to Alexander Technique as an instrumentalist, he was now planning to study strategies of self-use with a student of Jacques Lecoq's.

We both went to both of our classes—there were only a few areas of overlap. In his "Renaissance Humanism" lecture, he faced the professor while I looked toward the ground, practicing Spanish in my head. When I sat in my "Red, White, and Black in the Americas: The Initial Confrontation" seminar, I have no idea what he thought about.

We walked slowly and methodically, almost as though we were doing tai chi. We were so attuned, it was impossible to tell who led and who followed. We developed a strategy for kneeling while he positioned the cello off to his left, my right. We were one body and two bowing, twisting, forking heads.

It was an experiment in the plural body, which we saw as necessary research for understanding the possibilities of the collective body (as I mentioned earlier), or at least for understanding the limits of the physical individual. It seemed so clear that skin was porous and not a limit. Our physical selves had so many holes for a reason. They were not intended to be impenetrable. Hard as I was, mean as I was, I was not made of marble. Flesh was less solid than it seemed.

"I didn't mind," the philosopher said and stood up as though she were going to the window, or to get a glass of water, but she didn't go anywhere at all. She put a hand on her chair, as if to steady herself.

"The way we propped each other, were props for one another, she said. I didn't mind at all."

On my way out from the mall, I always paused at Auntie Anne's. Glossy and salty and yeasty like my own runny self. I would never actually absorb such a thing—basically wheat dust, held together with oil and leaven—but I liked to buy a giant pretzel just to carry, to feel the warmth in my palms. I held the mass softly with two hands as if they were the paws of a beloved. I loved slicking my fingers inside the bag, letting the warm bread cover and protect them.

Descending the escalator, people hustling past me on the right. I thought I was an island, but now I see that my shoulders have been rubbing and rubbing and rubbing again with the shoulders of strangers. I began to lean, ever so slightly, pow-ing people at regular intervals.

As I walked toward the exit, I touched the tip of someone's hand with mine on purpose; it left a thin, glistening streak. I wondered if they would wonder, later, why they shined.

A saxophone spreading in the distance.

Outside, I dropped small pieces of the pretzel on the ground as I walked. The outside was caramel-brown with dark striations, faux-char. It was white on the inside. I was like Goldilocks leaving a trail down Atlantic Avenue. For the birds, I thought.

The gist of the story was this: what we now think of as a person is actually only partial.

Or, put another way, every person had previously been plural. If you unfolded us, we might be like paper dolls, attached at the hand and foot. But the gods didn't treat us so gently. We were cleaved apart, our insides sucked and sealed at the navel.

If I closed my eyes, I could imagine it. I could be connected at the navel or the hip, or maybe the nubby tips of my fingers, to an-other. Maybe to the neighborhood association lady, or to all the teachers I'd ever had. To my mother and her mother. To Antwaun, to Antwaun's lover.

~

It was in the library that the philosopher and I had met. Not one of the university's many libraries, which I despised—too many restrictions, too clean, too quiet— but in the community library twenty blocks south.

I love all the tiptoeing and *shhhing*, the feeling of hallowed ground. Of course, the place is also a de facto community center, full of parents who need a break from the oppressive, dirty heat of their apartments, and men in proud, ill-fitting suits plucking out resumes with one finger on oversized greige computers, and grandmothers-turned-babysitters, their grandbabies reading in Spanish in the children's section, latchkey kids running wild. I had actually wanted to be a librarian as a young girl, but now I shudder to think of the danger, the dirty bathrooms, the constant policing. To be a librarian would require far too much talking.

The philosopher was numb to the weather, the way smokers and runners learn numbness, the way numbness is prerequisite and reward for exposing yourself to the elements. This was the first thing I knew we had in common. When I walked with leisure past the gate and through the front doors and passed a woman, ten feet from the entrance as legally required, holding a notebook that was getting soggier by the minute in one hand and a lit cigarette in the other, seemingly unaware that the heavens were crying, or sweating, or spitting, or pissing, or as she would later tell me (in one of the odd moments of spiritual connection), anointing her, and I recognized that look, the look of serene imperviousness, and registered it as I kept walking, and a few minutes or a few hours later, when I had been plodding away for some time on my ancient silver laptop, the j and f keys sticking to my damp fingers in the earthy humid light, feeling dimmer and greyer because of the rain outdoors, I saw her walk in, scraping her tote bags against the theft detectors and making her way in my general direction. She had a funny way of walking, not exactly limping but definitely stiff in the legs, as if moving from heel to heel without using her toes. But her hips were remarkably even and her shoulders proud and her back quite straight, so that the overall effect was one of the elegance of a marionette, or a princess used to being carried, or a very refined doll, and I was curious.

I hardened my shoulders and sat up in my chair, suddenly aware of the limitations of my posture. She sat down at the table next to mine, placed her things on the floor, and sat down carefully, a little gingerly, in a whiff of stale cigarettes which to me smelled like romance—it had been so long since I had known a smoker—and the kind of humidity that comes with someone who isn't afraid to sweat. Her skin was the color of walnut with a satin finish, burnished golden as if its age glowed her from the inside out; even from this distance of several feet, I could smell the cocoa butter. She paid no attention to the kids in the corner, or the day laborers plucking out resumes with one finger on the oversized beige computers, or the grandmothers-turned-babysitters, their grandbabies reading in Spanish in the children's section. She simply bent down over her black and white composition book and kept going for nearly two hours. When I came back after lunch at the bodega next door, she was still working solemnly and with urgency.

Excuse me. I heard a whisper from the table to my right. It was the marionette woman, looking intently at me with enormous black eyes. Her voice was actually quite elegant, not that I should been surprised. *How much does one of those things run?*

I blinked, looked around to see what she could be referring to. Books. Notes. She interrupted: *The computer. How much does one of those things run?*

I didn't know, I'd had it for years. But I think you can get one for a few hundred dollars, I told her.

Thank you, she said, and went back to her notebook. She was writing deliberately and with focus. I never once saw her look up.

Do you need to borrow it, I asked after a minute. *Can I do something for you?*

No, she said. *Well, I'm trying to get my book typed up, so I was thinking I should get a computer. But I can't type, not anymore.* She looked at my screen with interest.

Several weeks later, when I noticed a card on the community bulletin board: "Philosopher seeks typist for manuscript," it said. "$15/hour. Cash. Please call" etc., I knew, even before I called, who needed me.

~

I told her my name and she told me hers. She asked me again if I could type. We discussed scheduling and timing and location. We made contingency plans and exchanged phone numbers.

We did not initially discuss the content of the book, except in a very general sense: that it grew from her work as an actor in the 1970s, during which time she worked closely with a number of important artists whose ideas had never been adequately translated into English. She had entered graduate school in anthropology, technically, although she was really concerned with philosophical questions. But she had never finished her dissertation because her research, which took her to Paris, turned into exciting and pressing work as a dancer or dramaturge (it wasn't quite clear) and she let go of the reins, or maybe she herself was the horse moving in a new direction. Since returning to the U.S. in 1989, she had occasionally taught at community colleges but had never finished or tried to finish her degree, caring less about a credential these days, at her age, and more about the work. As she grew older it felt important to try to finish and publish a book, and she had learned about and written to a small independent press that specialized in books by women, which expressed interest but asked for a proposal and first chapter and, if possible, more. She was ready to prepare a draft but felt that the notes, as they lived in her notebook, were just too close. She hoped the activity of dictation, letting the words live between her and an other, would enable her to imagine the project as real. She felt that having a typing partner would provide some accountability and a schedule, as we would meet regularly, forcing her to write and read her revisions. She had very little to show for herself, when all was said and done, and she wanted this book to be the thing.

I nodded. We met, as we would often continue to meet, outside of a cafe, more of a deli really, with silver metal tables chained to the front door and chairs with horizontal vents that press stripes into your back.

At the deli, there is only one table and there are only two chairs, which means that when we meet, we are the only people who can sit for the time that we are working. Before we sat down, she had arranged the chairs so instead of facing each other, we were sitting nearly side by side facing the park, the storefront to our backs. As we sat, a young man walked back and forth between the basement storage—which could apparently only be accessed through corrugated metal doors that opened right onto the sidewalk—and the front door. We watched as he carried a large box of bananas, a box of canned beans, a giant black trash bag stuffed with apples.

When the details were clear, we stopped talking. A little while after that, I walked her all the way home. The soft pad of her Reeboks on the sidewalk, as we fell into step as though we had known one another for years.

The philosopher and I were a similar height and build. When I stood and she stood, my eyes were right at the level of hers. Our eyebrows, too, were at the same level, and our noses, and our mouths, and our necks. But we were not even all the way down. My breasts were higher than hers, and her legs were longer, and my feet were larger, and my hands were bigger, and she was louder, and I was probably needier, although I didn't even know it.

~

And then when we come to the end, we'll start again at the beginning, the philosopher reminded me often. *We'll complete an entire draft, and then a second, and then a third and final draft. I always write three drafts*, she said. *I don't want to labor it too much, you see*—and she re-crossed her legs with authority, as if the movement itself was an effort to convince.

A few months later she would tell me that "future me" might not believe in the same things as "me, of the moment—me, right now" because "we are only ever in the present in passing," and I still think of that feeling of being present in passing at the oddest times, but especially at Zumba, when I move and watch in the mirror as body after body moves. There is security in moving together.

I know there are birds, I think they're called swallows, that float in large masses, rarely flapping their wings, buoyed by the currents created around them. What does it feel like at the edge of the flock? Where you have to work so much harder than your neighbor to the right. What happens when you're safely in the middle and then suddenly the flock turns and you find yourself in front, flying harder, or in back, nearly left behind, or on the side, so easy to shear off or pick off?

Since I couldn't bring her to my dormitory, the philosopher and I often met outside. It was the most peaceful time of the day, sitting as I listened to her think, surrounded by the low hum of noise in the park across the street, the lilting voices of their mothers and shrieks of their children, comfortably separated by an avenue from our perch.

Sometimes, if it was raining, we would meet inside the house, smelling a little stale, filled with a funny combination of truly unique and very utilitarian furniture—the home of someone who can make home almost anywhere.

We would have a second or third coffee as we worked, and sometimes she would pull out cookies from her handbag—she liked the thin and crispy ones, the ones that tasted like winter spices. *I became addicted in Amsterdam*, she told me once, and I wondered what she knew about addiction. *Even now it feels a little barbaric to drink coffee without a little something sweet*, and I had never liked sweet things but I understood what she meant, even though I resented her for saying it. Before she came along, I had never found coffee bitter, and now I couldn't taste it without scrunching up my mouth. I began taking milk in my coffee where it had only been black before. She made so many things sharp that had only ever been smooth (and, to be fair, vice versa).

She baked bread every other day and cultivated yeast that she captured and grew from the air, she told me that she had kept this yeast alive for fourteen years, ever since the day before she moved into that house, so she kept a bit of her old house in her new house and ate it daily.

I never asked about the old house, about the time before she moved, and she didn't say much about her past, but there were hints to me of the possibility, the whiff, of another person in the house or in her life, someone who had shared her belongings.

There were things single people living alone don't often have, like an electric razor, and sometimes she would wear a baggy men's cardigan, so big it could have wrapped itself twice around her slight frame, and although she wore it casually and unsentimentally, I had a feeling that she was wrapping herself in someone else when she wore it, but I never asked, not really. I didn't know how to begin. Once I tried, I said, "You look like you're wrapped in someone else," just like that, and she tightened, I wouldn't call it a smile, and said nothing. But then I thought of my liturgical dance teacher, who wrapped nothing in mohair and called it grace.

She spoke her book as I typed. Every single word went into my ears and through my brain and out of my fingers. My residue clung to every piece. Gumming it? Greasing it? I felt—no, I knew—the book was thicker because it had been through my body.

I'm not embarrassed to admit that at the beginning and at the end, I disliked working for her.

I found the smell of rosewater that wafted where she went distasteful. I was annoyed by the slow deliberation with which she spoke and scornful of the way she overapplied her rouge. It scared me how when she coughed, it sounded like she was choking. I fumed when she asked me to get more napkins or a glass of water. (If I had learned anything from my parents, it was that I must not be anyone's servant, not on accident, not on purpose.)

It felt almost intolerable sometimes to wait for her to find a word on the tip of her tongue; once I suggested that I leave a few underscores to remind her to go back to that space during the revision and she was horrified, disgusted at the idea of emptiness in the manuscript, even for a few moments, as though I had suggested abandoning it altogether.

It was maddening the way she treated the copies I printed in the shared computer labs on campus. I wasn't allowed to bring guests into any of our buildings, so I would walk over to the nearest spot at the end of our sessions, do my business quickly, and walk back with the pages, her eyes watching me hungrily as I approached. She would carefully cover the sheaf with a rubber band and enclose it in a folder and place the folder in a shopping bag and then wrap the bag with both arms, like a precious child. And when she returned, the document marked up in her neat hand for revisions, it was always water ringed and crumbed and folded, as though she had been dragging it around for decades rather than days.

At the end of our hours together, I would go back to my dorm or back to the library, back to my assignments, back to my classes, and I felt as if I were going back to juvenilia itself. I rolled my eyes at my classmates with their CK One, drinking, swooning over boys. They thought they were smart, arguing about Washington and Du Bois, pretending they cared about wars they would never see, saying things like "existence precedes essence" as if their essence was ever under threat.

~

But I didn't stop because I disliked her. I stopped because increasingly often, when I was supposed to be writing my own assignments, I found myself sitting quietly in front of the keyboard, hands lightly touching the keys, in a ready position. I got into the habit of waiting for the words to come to me, to be spoken to me, the way she spoke to me.

It wasn't long before I realized that her soft and steady voice was always present underneath, as long as I was quiet enough to listen.

I became so attached to her voice inside my head that I actually felt lonely without it. I started to avoid loud places. I stopped going to the campus cafeteria, which I used to frequent even into my sophomore and junior years, preferring meals that were made for me over fighting for space in the shared dorm room kitchen. I skipped the rowdy meeting sessions of certain large clubs, like the Black Student Union, which I never really liked anyway. I even started staying away from the frisbee-filled college quad on certain sunny days.

The problem was that solitude, for me, was like a light beer to an alcoholic, a gateway drug that tasted way too sweet. I was playing with fire, and I knew it. Because I had never become what you'd call chatty, but by college I spoke when spoken to and could keep a conversation going when necessary. Because it was important to participate, even if most of it was babble. Because at the end of the day, at the end of the year, at the end of my life, I didn't want to be alone.

Sometimes when I was feeling fanciful, I imagined myself not so much a word processor as a word metabolizer, a word converter, a word compressor, turning what was whole and round into pixels and light.

The problem began when I started to wonder whether any letters, in any order, could ever be "mine."

I mean, who am I to say when anything begins or when anything ends or whether it matters.

～

Nothing surprises me now.
  Déja vu. Already seen.
  Vis-à-vis. Whose face to whose face.

～

I was thinking of the library and the philosopher when I searched the digital card catalog for "stop gripping."

I found a title about horseback riding and how to avoid using your knees for stability, one about golf clubs, one about video games and the way you hold the mouse ("death grip"), one about violin technique and how you hold the bow, one about bowling, several about Brazilian Jiu-Jitsu, one about death metal guitar technique, one about masturbation, and one about Pilates. With some skepticism, I ordered the Pilates and masturbation ones through interlibrary loan. The Pilates arrived first.

It turned out to be less about healing and releasing and more about how to tighten the right muscles and loosen the others in order to build strength in a targeted way. The author had studied with a student of one of Joseph Pilates's students and wrote with clear authority. The book was organized almost like a cookbook, with lots of individual exercises and little narrative introductions to each section. Most of these were almost like diary entries, saying how the author was reminded of X technique while standing on a cliff in England, or learned to let go of Y technique while on safari in South Africa.

The recipes didn't work, not for me. I'm not good at self-soothing. Somebody else has to soothe me.

Come to think of it, the masturbation title never arrived at all.

It was winter, so I had to get my iced coffee in a bottle pre-sweetened, and I prefer to drink it black. But sugary iced coffee is better than no iced coffee at all, and I need some kind of hit, some boost of intensity to get me past the threshold of the YMCA, past the gnarled man who manages the convoluted scanning and ticketing and entry system, his presence nothing but a kink in what could have been a smooth entry, past the antiseptic smell of the hallway and the speckled linoleum floor, past the heavy metal doors and into the funk and noise of the gym itself, where I have to slide along the edges of the room on the other side of the caution line taped in red, slinking past the dozens of people sitting at stations covered in sweat, a towel behind their backs or around their necks, staring at their cell phones as if the act of looking was so different, so painful, that it caused that shiny goo to emanate from their leaky pores, past the people who stare at the opaque diagrams on the side of each machine, grab the nearest dangling handle, and try moving it, and it's too easy or too hard, and their elbows look awkward and their backs aren't quite right and their shoulders are shrugged but they're still doing something, aren't they?

I pass, slightly ashamed, one among a line of us who are not yet sweating, who are mostly women, who aren't moving heavy things except their own bodies, and our bodies weigh on us very heavily indeed.

~

I joined this wretched place by necessity, not by choice. I wasn't supposed to run, as you know. I had to convalesce, the doctor had said.

But I found myself fidgeting all morning, every morning, itchy and cold.

I ate, but I took no pleasure in food.

I would lace up my shoes (for comfort, I told myself) and plan to walk to the park (to rest, I told myself).

And the walk would inevitably slide into a jog (just until the end of the block, I said), which would begin with the blissful knowledge that the pain was gone— it was as if I had never stopped—it was as good as it has ever been—is how I would feel. And that bliss would drop deeper and deeper into my stomach until it reached what has been called the "pit," and as my stomach sank, a distant ache got nearer and nearer, as though I were running toward it, as though the pain itself were the corner, and then when I reached it and crossed it and went to the other side, the pain was no longer approaching but already all around me, like an unpleasant street that I had to run through in order to get out.

Sometimes I would try changing my stride, running faster, thinking mathematically about ankles and angles and gravity and force, and sometimes it would help for a few seconds, probably just a distraction, and then it would return deep as ever, sometimes so deep it would take my breath away, and I would even stumble and trip, and go back to walking, but by then even walking was painful, so I would often just stand, come to an entire standstill on the side of the sidewalk and then make my way, gingerly, heel to heel, back around the block to my home. And I knew that my fantasy—that things were already better—was actually making everything worse.

But lord, I was restless. Too much surplus energy. I tried doing calisthenics at home, sit-ups and pushups and stuff, but got bored.

One afternoon, after a particularly rough morning in which I had talked my way out of running but couldn't stop myself from moping, I decided on a whim to enter the local YMCA, which, as I mentioned, faced the park directly. It was a rush, the smell of bleach and chlorine and sweat, and I soaked it in for a few moments.

"Can I help you," the lady said, and I asked for a schedule of classes, fully prepared to pretend to look. But then it was actually interesting, this list. Maybe there would be a viable alternative to running here. Vinyasa yoga. Indoor cycling. Total body conditioning.

"What's Zumba?" I asked her, not because I didn't already have a pretty good idea, but because I wanted to hear somebody try to describe it without sounding ridiculous.

"Girl, it's fun. You have to try it. It's not hard at all." She shimmied in her seat. "You follow the instructor, and she does a little routine, and you do it too. And there's music. Get yourself a good sweat."

I was not convinced.

"Anybody can do it, really. The class is full of little old ladies and regular women, just having some fun. Even some youth sometimes will be in there. Hell, I'll even hop in there sometimes and you know I can't dance."

I thought about it.

"Do you like Cyndi Lauper?" she asked. "I love that, when Miss Jackson plays 'Girls Just Want to Have Fun'. Miss Jackson's the teacher—she used to be a real dancer on Broadway. So trim, too. Looking fine as hell at fifty and then some." She winked. "You know how we do."

I was skeptical at first. My favorite things to do were outside, and this was stiflingly enclosed. I had never even belonged to a gym. Ignoring Addy, I signed up for a class called Bodypump, which involved lifting light-to-medium-sized weights in rhythm with others. I was shocked to realize how weak I was—sometimes even the five-pound weights were too much for me to handle—and

I resolved to use this time away from running to get stronger.

But on my way out, I would see the women for Zumba coming in. They were so light on their feet, not self-righteous, grinning.

For my first Zumba class, I found myself a spot in the back. The women around me flailed and sweated and I just stood there, quietly, watching. I didn't move a muscle. I was not animated by this music, a mix of Cyndi Lauper, Janet Jackson, and whatever popular hits didn't have too much cursing. There were other black women in the room—it was a YMCA in East New York, after all—but they were *getting down* in a way that, for me, required a few drinks and the cover of darkness. At the end the teacher gave me a funny glance—I had barely moved since I walked in the door—but said nothing.

I don't know why I decided to come back.

It was social, and running was private. It was enclosed, and running was wide open, free. But the things they had in common were more important than those they didn't share. In Zumba, I could move continuously, none of the starting and stopping of Bodypump. Zumba offered the pleasure of studying a whole room full of people. The routines, I soon discovered, were almost the same every class, which meant my mind was free to wander to the other people in the room. Not unlike the way my mind wandered when running. I could modify the jumping to protect my shins, substituting little *pliés* when I needed to. Most importantly, it was something to look forward to, at a time when my pain-filled days felt both cold, bleak, and fairly empty. Unlike Bodypump, Zumba was offered every day of the week.

~

I slide through the door and up the stairs to the balcony, the rubber and sweat smell mixing well, I think, with the flavor of my coffee, hidden in my bag. And then I sit in another hallway where the women gather, pacing and stretching, a kind of nervous energy, and then the door opens and a jumble of ponytails and fluorescents and purple cheeks spills out and when it trickles to a near stop, we enter and see a straggler or two speaking animatedly to the instructor, who looks hot and in a hurry but also patient as she listens to someone explain about the pain in their pinkie toe, which means they can come back but can't really move their feet, at least not for another few months until the bunion is healed, and does she have any suggestions for modifications, and I almost smile as I think about my achy shins.

We all shuffle in and I watch as some pretend to touch their toes, or focus as they try to do crunches, cramming in an entire other workout before the workout we're here to do together. The room has a ballet barre running all the way around it—in the evenings, it's used to teach ballet to kids—and I lean against the bar, using it as a prop to stretch my shoulders while I watch the instructor for my class fiddle with her iPod as all of us get settled in our favorite corners of the room, which she recognizes by now.

When the music starts, I am ready, feet shoulder width apart, head ready to roll right and left and center, less ready to march in step with other marching legs like a deranged soldier, and I actually think this is the closest I will ever feel to being a military man, kicking my butt with my heels to a beat, my body feels positively well ordered, more organized than it has been all day, and I find my gaze softening as I absorb not what any one person is doing, but rather the group and its movements as a single organism, as if we were a school of fish or an octopus with many synchronized legs.

There is one person who likes to be in the front row, whose energy breaks the energy of the group because it is so excessive. When the instructor hops gracefully, she bounds like a basketball player, coming down with a thump. It takes longer to jump so high—her airtime is really remarkable—and with each landing she is later and later to the beat, until finally she is so far behind that she has to skip a few steps to catch up, and her furrowed forehead, the jumble in her face and in her step, shows how mad she is that even though she's doing it right—she thinks bigger is right—she is being punished by being left behind, as though it were our fault and not hers. She is a bit younger than the other women, maybe college-aged, maybe used to always getting it right, and I can see that this dissonance is really upsetting to her, that she can't be her best here except by being the same as us all. Indeed, a few months later I will see her downstairs in the weight room, looking like her back might break against the strain of the barbell, being barked at and then soothed by a middle-aged woman who clearly understands her sadomasochistic inner life.

There is someone who takes the class in a sweatshirt and some kind of corset, which is supposed to winnow her stomach while leaving her breasts and ass intact. She sometimes covers herself with a kind of garbage bag with a hood to produce even more sweat, which looks so oily on her skin, pooling with her heavy foundation, that I can see how she mistakes it for fat cells weeping directly from her pores.

There is one man. Always only one man.

The music was Bruno Mars. I was focused on my arms—kick and kick and punch and punch and—and we were turning to the beat, and as I faced the rear corner I saw her out from the edge of my eye, kicking.

I could sense her even before I could see her directly. I think it was her posture, which was very particular. Pulled up, as if someone had told her to gather up her skeleton and order it from top to bottom, just as she had stood with her dog's leash in her hand at the threshold of her door, as if she were holding her breath.

I kept turning, and soon I was facing the mirror again, and if I squinted I could almost see her. But I quickly realized that I could either look at the woman or perform the movements, but not both.

Every time we faced the back of the room, I saw her head.

When we *chasséed* left, I could see a glimpse of her shoulders.

So here we were, not meeting, not touching, but rather operating in a kind of permanent parallel. Barely visible to one another. No one ever talks about the intimacy of parallel, like the intimacy between siblings, next to one another in straight lines that can never cross, or the intimacy of your street and your neighbor's street that run side by side and never touch.

When the song ended, and the next song ended, and the next song ended, there was a short water break. I never brought water—a sign of weakness, I thought, plus I didn't like to see my stomach bloated in the mirror, plus I didn't like the feeling of it sloshing around as I hopped. I thought I'd try to make eye contact again—would she remember me?—but she was buried in her bag and didn't look up.

Class went on for nearly an hour.

The thought of her eyes looking at me from the back was disconcerting. I was glad I'd worn my baggiest shirt, my most flattering leggings.

Yes, she looked like me. But she didn't dance like me.

By the end, I was shedding sweat from all sides, panting like a dog, but the woman looked serene. We were about a mile from her house: not far, by New York terms, but not right next door either. I wondered if she would change in the locker room? But no, I watched as she put on a light vest and draped her bag across her chest. I scrambled, while pretending not to scramble, to get ready quickly. I wanted to happen to head out with her, then happen to head in the same direction, and then somehow start a conversation—about what, I had no idea.

She was already past the entrance and on her way toward the exit, dilly-dallying with no one on her way out, just a smile and nod to the instructor who, as the front desk had promised, was indeed a former chorus girl. I wondered why I'd never seen the woman in class before, even though I'd been coming nearly every day for weeks.

～

Years ago, the philosopher had taught me how to rush without looking like I was rushing. She walked slowly herself—knees—but she showed me her ways. Pretend that the wind is pushing your hips forward, she would say. In other words, use your core rather than your legs to glide you. It's a good trick, and I was able to use it today to stay very close even though she was practically sprinting through the weight room and against the turnstiles and into the wave of hot air, and we were already hot, or at least I was, having been moving in that hot room for at least 57 minutes straight.

I played it so that we "happened" to wait at the corner to cross Arlington Road together for the entire length of the light, at least twenty seconds. I considered what I should say. Something about her dog? The article?

The weather?

    "Did—" I almost said.

    "Hel—" I almost said.

    "Wh—" I almost said.

    But nothing came out, just some big preparatory breaths, and by the time I figured out how to speak, the stoplight had changed and I let her leave.

A Rock, A River, A Street

This time I saw a deer in a parking lot as big as a football field behind the art museum in my hometown, and how it froze when looking at me and how I froze when looking at it

This time my class went to the zoo in second or third grade—sometime when I wasn't speaking—they passed around a tiny animal, a mongoose or a lemur or a muskrat (now I'm just making things up, I actually have no idea what the animal was) and it was petrified, scared nearly (I think) to death, so that even as it was frozen, it was continuously shitting little hard pellets as we handed it, one to the other, like mammal BBs

fear-fear-fear-fear-fear-
fear-fear-fear-fear-fear-fear-fear-fear-fear

I went to class at the church weekly, faithfully. My teacher would tell me to take a deep breath, the deepest of the day, the deepest of the week, the deepest of my entire life.

I would look around me with my eyes—my body was immobile—and, even seeing what there was to see, even knowing what it was, I would let it all in.

Your shins, my teacher told me, are not damaged but blocked.

The blockage originates in your throat. Did you now that your throat is perfectly aligned with the shin from front to back, she asked? Have you ever been blocked in the throat? she asked.

We would face one another, each lying on a mat, her on her left side and me on my right. *Repeat after me*, she would say, but what she meant was *do as I do*.

She made intricate patterns with her arms and legs, like a magician. I followed, like a hare. I realized that the tiniest gestures can have an extraordinary impact. That a centimeter to the right here, a millimeter to the back there, a bracing here and a loosening there, could be the difference between living with pain and living without it.

Bones terminate in capsules, she said. *We have to dissolve the joint capsule to find mobility, like dissolving the outer layer of a pill.*

Why are we lying?, I asked

One shin at a time, she said.

I would frantically scan her body, looking for difference. I saw her foot in the air and moved my foot to match it. I saw her arm overturn, elbow upward, and turned my own arm to match. I saw her fold in on herself and I followed.

I followed, I tried to follow. And yet I knew I was missing so much. If I watched her ankle to get exactly the right angle, I missed what her neck was doing. If I looked at her neck, I missed the shift of her hip.

Over time, I came to recognize that everything I needed was in her eyes. I would stare directly at her pupils for minutes, hours. I imagined I could see my own self reflected in their curves. In her eyes, I could track every little thing she did. She would stare back, equally intent. Without breaking eye contact, she would say "You missed a turn" or "use your core to bring your toe toward your navel" or "soften your ribs" or simply "breathe."

She laid her hands on me and I whimpered.

She laid her hands on me and I growled, and the growl sometimes turned into a roar.

She laid her hands on me and I sighed, and the sigh sometimes turned into a cough.

She laid her hands on me and I hiccupped.

She laid her hands on me and I yawned.

She laid her hands on me and I had to avert my eyes.

She laid her hands on me and I had to close my eyes.

She laid her hands on me and I had to squeeze my eyes closed.

She laid her hands on me and tears came to my eyes and dripped from my nose and down the back of my throat and I coughed again.

She laid her hands on me and I sneezed.

She laid her hands on me and I held my breath.

She laid her hands on me and I grunted a few times.

She laid her hands on me and I hummed involuntarily.

She laid her hands on me and I let out a slow sound from the back of my throat, like when the dentist tells you to say *aaaaah*, but quieter.

She laid her hands on me and I smiled, which sometimes turned into a giggle.

She laid her hands on me and I gagged and flung them back off.

Some days were better than others.

One day I made the mistake of mentioning to my teacher how sweet it was to miss running, how juicy and full my heart felt with the absence, and she narrowed her eyes.

What do you run from, she said, and then put a hand up to shush.

Don't tell me here, and she touched her own throat. *Tell me here*, and she gestured at my body, a swipe from crown to toe.

"You know what I remembered?" she told me. "That the word *shin* comes from a word that means *thin*. Thin piece." Isn't that something? Thin piece. It could just as well describe any bone.

"Shin like shim," I said. Also a thin piece.

"Like shingle," she said. A thin covering.

"Like shit," I said. A piece of me.

"Like skim," she said. The thinnest milk.

"Like scissors," I said. To slice.

"Like shiver," I said. A little shake.

"Like schism," she said. A break.

From themselves
From the police
In circles
To the point
-away
Into your arms
In their sleep
-on sentences
From their sins
From their pasts
In place
For charity
For your heart muscles
For your leg muscles
To clear your head
To beat somebody else

A Rock, A River, A Street

One time, I won't say when, I wanted to rush but she
wouldn't be rushed, so we walked slowly, hip to hip,
buzzed a grey buzzer, walked again up three sets of
stairs, past a micro theater, past a Broadway rehearsal
studio, and then we were in the light, in an impossibly
sunny room with a skylight and a wall of crusted windows and an old maple floor with a yellowing finish
and a wall covered with a red velvet curtain so dusty
and faded that it was the color of my brown forearm.
There were white women everywhere, in sweatpants
and harem pants and some kind of stretchy-looking
khakis, and a few in leggings and tunics and tank tops,
each breast floating in a different direction as they lazily
stretched one leg over another, rolled out a hip, lay on
their backs with their feet straight up in the air, rocked
backward and forward on their heels. We joined them,
relaxing into our forward folds, our knees soft, carefully
releasing our heads and closing our eyes, wrangling into
a pigeon pose, feeling a sinewy tug from the back of the
buttocks, feeling it give way at the knee.

We waited and stretched in silence, and then the
teacher began to speak, she was talking in a regular
voice, just telling us what a beautiful day it was, how
nice and sunny, how nice to feel our bodies vibrating
and opening, do we feel that vibration, listen closely
for it. Doesn't it seem like listening is the way to tune
our bodies, to become open and receptive from our
fingers to our toes, and if you listen hard enough you'll
hear your own blood flowing, and it flows smooth like a

river, and the smooth river flowing current of your fluid blood is rushing and streaking and bubbling through your body, and that rhythm, it's one you can tap into, you can feel the rush and flow in it, and let that begin to animate your body from the inside to the outside, so that your fingers are moving a little from the rush, your toes are moving, your ankles and wrists are flowing, your forearms and calves are flowing, your knees, your elbows, your upper arms, your thighs, your shoulders, your pelvis, your neck, your core, your collarbone, your abdomen, and then they converge, they converge at your heart, everything is flowing from and to the heart, and as you feel the flow through your limbs begin to undulate them, push them, help your body flow the blood, push harder, imagine your insides rattling and leaking and bloody and come back to stillness. And now in the stillness notice your little movements, and make them a little bigger, and now bigger and bigger, and begin to shake, shake your head on your own neck, shake at the knees, and as you shake slowly flow and leak your body upward into the air, upward into the room, let yourself leak toward others, you're spilling, you're leaking, you're leaking on your neighbor. Flutter your eyes closed. Flutter your eyes open. Leaking onto your neighbor. How does it feel to be leaked onto? Are you feeling your flow melding into your neighbor's? Is it strengthening them, like a transfusion, a transfusion of energy, like your blood is flowing from you to your neighbor, and they're a vampire, and they're feeding on you, let the energy drain from you and enter someone else. What does it feel like to be drained? For the other partner, let yourself be nourished by your neighbor. How can you get enough of them? Can you ever get enough of them? How can you absorb them? How are you gradually strengthening as they weaken? You are feeding, being nourished and nourishing, held together in the same word. You are growing, you are getting thicker, your muscles are getting stronger, your tendons are thickening, you are feeling enriched, you are getting fatter and heavier. You have fed too much. You begin flowing back to your partner. You are restoring equilibrium. Can you find equilibrium with each other? You are each putting weight on each other. You are each to each from each to each from each to each from each. You are becoming closer and closer. You are one. How much of your weight can you share with the other person? What does it feel like to let go? To hold and be held? Isn't it such a gift? Isn't it such a pleasure? To know that you are alone and not responsible for holding yourself up? That someone can do it with you? For you? Maybe that someone is a stranger. Maybe it's someone you know very well. What tenderness is it, to hold someone's head in your hands? What safety to allow yourself to be held? To allow someone to hold your wrist and support your wrist? To allow someone to hold your pinky and support your pinky? How delicate is your pinky? Think of how much power they have, how much power you're giving them, as they hold your smallest digit that is no less precious for its smallness. Allow yourself to withdraw your pinky. Allow the other person to hold their own fingers. How does it feel to support your own self entirely? Can you support yourself and feel the support of others? Can you feel both at the same time? Move with that support? Begin with your pinky—move it with the strength, the trust, that you built when someone was supporting you. Extend that to your palm. To your other fingers. To the delicate joint where your hand meets your arm. To the delicate place where your arm bends. It is now supported. Can you feel that support? To the delicate place where your clavicle cradles the socket of your shoulder? To your skinny, bony, hole-y spine, your holy spine. Supported. Fully supported by your partner even thought they are no longer physically holding you. They're there and you feel them strengthening and buttressing your back, and your femurs and your shins, strong bones made even stronger and more powerful with your partner's support. You can do anything. You can go anywhere. You find yourself capable of things you didn't even know were possible. You are bending. You are jumping. You have power because it is as if your partner is supporting and strengthening and lifting and boosting you. You're stronger and bigger. You're taking up more space. You're roaring. Doesn't it feel great? And now your movements are powerful but smaller, all the power compressed into a smaller gesture. The power is inside. It is hidden but present as you walk around the room and make eye contact with others. They can feel it, you can feel it in them. You are not wary of their hidden power, you trust it in others because you trust it in yourself. You are yourself amplified. You are walking more slowly, still holding and staring and with an exquisite awareness of your strength. You are coming to a stop. You are getting still. Your stillness is your strength. You are sharing strength with every single person in this room.

I had spent the entire class, from beginning to end, touching her. I had felt her thin skin, the collagen and cells and body oil and flakes that were all over me now.

The sunlight came in harsh, but the dust and dirt on the windows and in the room gave it a soft filter, like Kodachrome.

There was one point, when her pinky was cradled in my hand, that I felt almost ecstatic with intimacy. Her eyes were looking at me carefully and openly and not at all harshly, and I felt almost like mamas do with their babies, like they could literally eat them, I could eat her and it wouldn't be enough, there would always be a ridge, a wrinkle, a joint, a break. And I opened my mouth slightly to open up for the dust I could see streaming through the window beams, the dust of generations of bodies, her dust. And when the cells dripped in? I closed my eyes and waited, even though I already knew:

Things I have seen on my runs and in my walks: that the driveway to the cemetery was not paved, but strewn with small stones. Most of the stones were white, but a very few were dark grey.

    To do something stonely.
    To do something stonily.
    To do something stonelike.

Things I have seen in my walks: outside the McDonalds, an unusual bush. The surface was mottled: some leaves were dark green, as if shaded, and others were the color of spring, as if sunny. When I looked more closely, I saw what I thought was a single tree was actually two plants entangled. One had grown into and through the other.

The color of polished walnut, but the polish expired
years ago
    the inside of an M&M, bitten and exposed
    a strip of faded burlap, weave darkened and loosened
in patches
    a certain kind of stucco, rougher than brownstone
    a certain kind of cracker, grainy, half crumbled
    recycled cardboard, as if I myself have been pressed
    cracked leather, as if I myself have been skinned

ACKNOWLEDGMENTS

To everyone at Primary Information, especially my very patient editor, Rachel Valinsky.

To Sarah, K-Sue, Kristen, Alex, Jenny, Annie, Zoë, Taylor Renee, and the writers at Louis Place.

To Erica, Sahra, Andrea, Anjuli, Thomas, Alex, Carol, Taylor, Natalie, Marc, Rezarta, Amanda, and many other colleagues, friends, and interlocutors.

To the Guggenheim Foundation and the Creative Capital Foundation, for financial assistance during the writing period.

To my family—Phyllis, Steve, Philip, and Jaslyn.

To Quincy Flowers, whose unwavering support made this book possible.

A Rock, A River, A Street
© 2022 Steffani Jemison

ISBN: 978-1-7365346-6-3

Images: *Untitled (Stroke 1–10)*, 2022. Courtesy of the artist.

Editor: Rachel Valinsky

Designer: Pacific
Elizabeth Karp-Evans & Adam Turnbull

Copy Editor: Mayra A. Rodríguez Castro

Primary Information
232 3rd St, #A113
The Old American Can Factory
Brooklyn, NY 11215
www.primaryinformation.org

Printed by Versa Press

This book is made possible, in part,
by the generous support of Greene Naftali Gallery.

Primary Information is a 501(c)(3) non-profit organization that receives
generous support through grants from the Michael Asher Foundation,
Empty Gallery, the Graham Foundation for Advanced Studies in the
Fine Arts, the Greenwich Collection Ltd, the John W. and Clara C.
Higgins Foundation, the Willem de Kooning Foundation, the Henry
Luce Foundation, Metabolic Studio, the National Endowment for
the Arts, the New York City Department of Cultural Affairs in
partnership with the City Council, the New York State Council on
the Arts with the support of Governor Andrew Cuomo and the
New York State Legislature, the Orbit Fund, the Stichting Egress
Foundation, Teiger Foundation, The VIA Art Fund, The Jacques
Louis Vidal Charitable Fund, The Andy Warhol Foundation for the
Visual Arts, the Wilhelm Family Foundation, and individuals worldwide.